S0-AYF-772

J-FICTION

Goddess Girls

SUPER SPECIAL
THE GIRL GAMES

READ ALL THE BOOKS IN THE

GODDESS GIRLS SERIES

Athena the Brain

Persephone the Phony

Aphrodite the Beauty

Artemis the Brave

Athena the Wise

Aphrodite the Diva

Artemis the Loyal

Medusa the Mean

Goddess Girls

SUPER SPECIAL
THE GIRL GAMES

JOAN HOLUB & SUZANNE WILLIAMS

Aladdin

NEW YORK LONDON TORONTO SYDNEY NEW DELHI

ALADDIN
An imprint of Simon & Schuster Children's Publishing Division
1230 Avenue of the Americas, New York, NY 10020
First Aladdin paperback edition July 2012
Copyright © 2012 by Joan Holub and Suzanne Williams
All rights reserved, including the right of reproduction
in whole or in part in any form.
ALADDIN is a trademark of Simon & Schuster, Inc., and related logo
is a registered trademark of Simon & Schuster, Inc.
For information about special discounts for bulk purchases,
please contact Simon & Schuster Special Sales at 1-866-506-1949
or business@simonandschuster.com.
The Simon & Schuster Speakers Bureau can bring authors to your live event.
For more information or to book an event contact the Simon & Schuster Speakers
Bureau at 1-866-248-3049 or visit our website at www.simonspeakers.com.
Designed by Karin Paprocki
The text of this book was set in Baskerville Handcut Regular.
Manufactured in the United States of America 0812 OFF
2 4 6 8 10 9 7 5 3
Library of Congress Control Number 2012932940
ISBN 978-1-4424-4933-6
ISBN 978-1-4424-4934-3 (eBook)

Goddess Girls

SUPER SPECIAL
THE GIRL GAMES

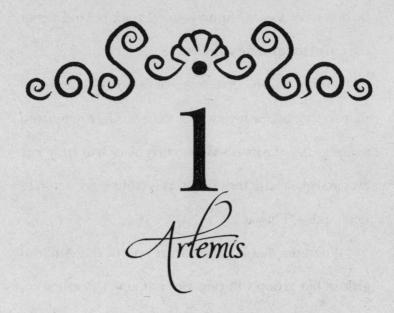

1

Artemis

Thursday morning.

WE ARE STANDING IN THE COURTYARD OF Mount Olympus Academy," a goddessgirl named Artemis announced to the tour group gathered around her. The seven girls in her group, who were visiting MOA for the next few days, followed her gaze. The majestic academy— built of gleaming white stone and surrounded on all sides by dozens of Ionic columns—stood right behind her at the top of the granite staircase.

Pointing down, Artemis continued, "The white marble tiles beneath your feet were brought here from a quarry in"—she brushed her curly black hair from her eyes and glanced at the official MOA tour guide scroll in her hands—"Thasos."

"Wherever *that* is," she heard one of the Amazon girls in her group whisper. Her name was Penthesilea. Dozens of silver bracelets jangled noisily on her arms as she moved. Another Amazon girl, named Hippolyta, smacked the gum she was chewing and shrugged.

Ye gods! Why did I have to get these two mean Amazon girls in my group? Artemis wondered. They wore platform sandals, stood ten inches taller than any of the other girls, and were known for being bold and brash. Still, they didn't have to be rude!

Artemis's goddessgirl friend, Persephone, sent her an encouraging smile. She was helping lead the group and was always trying to make sure everyone got along.

"Remember," Persephone whispered to her. "These girls have traveled a long way to get here from schools on Earth and other realms. They're tired and probably anxious about the Games this Saturday. So let's cut them some slack."

Artemis nodded. In truth, she couldn't really blame the Amazons for being a teeny bit bored. They'd come to take part in the very-first-ever girls-only Olympic Games. Only two days away! A thrill of excitement shot up her spine at the thought of the upcoming competitions.

Although everybody was calling them the Girl Games, their official name was the *Heraean* Games. Zeus, the principal of MOA, had named them after his new wife, Hera. And it was Hera's idea to have MOA students give these tours to visiting girl athletes.

It was a good idea, Artemis supposed. The problem was that she didn't really have time to play tour guide. She had too much other stuff to do to get ready for the Games. Like her, these girls would probably rather be off practicing for their own athletic events right now. After all, there wasn't much time left!

Noticing that Artemis had gone quiet, Persephone took over as tour guide for a while. "Let's go look inside the Academy next," she suggested to their group. Her long, wavy red hair brushed her pale arm as she turned and led them all up the granite staircase.

Artemis followed, her mind full of the megazillion tasks she still needed to do to make sure that everything on Game Day would go off without a hitch. These girls-only Olympics had been her idea, and she didn't want them to bomb. How awful would that be?

Her stomach tightened as she pushed through the enormous bronze doors of the Academy. Just thinking about the possibility of failure stressed her out. Everyone was counting on her.

An awed silence fell over the girls in their group as they filed inside, entering the main hall. Persephone went over to a golden fountain against one wall. She turned it on for a second so that glittery liquid spurted from its spout in an arc.

"Instead of water, the fountains here at MOA spout nectar," she said.

"That's what Immortals drink to make their skin shimmer, right?" interrupted a mortal girl in their group. "What would happen if I drank it?"

"Nothing. It has no effect on mortals," answered a green-skinned mortal MOA student passing by.

Medusa. She and another mortal girl named Pandora were leading a tour group of six girls.

Medusa was wearing her stoneglasses, which were sort of like sunglasses. Without them, her gaze would have turned Pandora and every other mortal she gazed upon to stone. Including the Amazons.

Hey, maybe that wouldn't be such a bad thing! Artemis thought, grinning to herself.

"Isn't this the most awesome school ever?" Pandora asked her and Medusa's group. Then, without waiting for an answer, she fired off more questions. "Did you notice how the domed ceiling overhead is covered with paintings celebrating the exploits of Olympic gods and goddesses? And see that one with Zeus battling giants as they storm Mount Olympus carrying spears and torches? Doesn't it just give you the shivers?"

As a fitting symbol of her curiosity—and constant

questions—Pandora's blue bangs were plastered against her forehead in the shape of question marks.

"Are any of you swimmers?" Artemis heard Medusa ask as the group continued down the hall. A few girls nodded. "Then you'll be competing in the Games with me," she informed them. "And," she added slyly, "my snakes."

On cue, her snake hair writhed and hissed, making the other girls step back warily. All except one of the Chinese girls, who said, "No problem. I like snakes."

As Medusa, Pandora, and their tour group rounded the corner and went out of sight, three of MOA's cutest godboys entered the front hall from the other direction: Ares, Poseidon, and Apollo. As soon as they saw the new girls, they began to show off.

Ares flexed his muscles. Poseidon twirled his trident (a three-pronged spear) over his head. And Apollo, who was Artemis's twin brother, flashed his widest smile and waved.

Artemis rolled her eyes. She was just about to shoo them all away when a mortal boy came to join them—Actaeon. Seeing him, her face grew hot. He was her crush. She wasn't totally sure he liked her, and she didn't know if he knew she liked him either. It was all very complicated.

Feeling weirdly shy, she looked away from him. Her eyes happened to fall on one of the Amazons—Penthesilea, who was staring from her to Actaeon and back again. Catching Artemis's gaze, she smirked knowingly.

"Ooh! Those MOA boys are *so* cute," Penthesilea cooed. "Especially that mortal one. Right, Hippolyta?" She elbowed her friend.

Hippolyta smacked the pine gum she was chewing,

her expression a mixture of surprise and confusion. "Uh, yeah, sure. I guess so."

Grrr. Artemis glared at them. Amazons had the reputation of being sports-crazy, not boy-crazy. So why was Penthesilea suddenly acting so ga-ga over Actaeon?

Ares and Poseidon decided to head down the hall after Pandora and Medusa's tour group. But Apollo and Actaeon broke away and came over to Artemis's group. Penthesilea's bracelets clanked as she ran a hand over her short brown hair. She smiled at Actaeon and he smiled back.

"Back off. Actaeon's *my* crush!" Artemis told her. Well, she didn't say it out loud, of course—just in her head.

"How's it going, sis?" Apollo asked.

"Hi, Artemis," Actaeon said at the same time.

At the sound of the boys' voices, Penthesilea pretended to swoon. The quick-thinking Actaeon caught

her before she could hit the marble floor. Unfortunately.

"Thanks," Penthesilea murmured, smiling up at him
and batting her eyelashes.

What a faker! thought Artemis.

But Actaeon just grinned at the Amazon girl. "Sure.
Anytime."

Apollo's eyebrows rose. "Whoa! I've never had a
girl faint at the sight of me. Usually they run away." It
was true. Her brother's first crush was a nymph who'd
turned herself into a laurel tree rather than tell him she
didn't like him.

Actaeon slapped him on the back. "Maybe things are
looking up for you, god-dude," he said with a grin.

It was nice of him to say that, thought Artemis. Only,
she was pretty sure that it was Actaeon rather than
Apollo that Penthesilea had pretended to swoon for.

"I'm Penthesilea," the Amazon girl informed Actaeon in a high, flirty voice. "But you can call me Penthe. What's your name?"

Artemis's fist closed around her guide scroll, crushing the middle of it flat. Noticing her reaction, Persephone quickly stepped between Penthe and the boys. "That's Actaeon," she piped up, pointing at the mortal boy. "And this is Artemis's brother, Apollo."

Good thing Persephone was a pro at jumping in to smooth over awkward situations, thought Artemis.

Persephone's introductions gave Artemis time to take a deep breath. Principal Zeus had said that part of the purpose of the Games was to promote a friendly cultural exchange. They were supposed to be on their best behavior. So, beaning Penthe over the head with her tour guide scroll probably wouldn't be the best way to impress Zeus. And it definitely wouldn't promote goodwill among cultures! Artemis relaxed her fist.

Boom! Boom! Boom!

Godzooks! Speaking of Principal Zeus, here he came now, stomping down the hall toward them wearing a dazzling white tunic and golden sandals. The girls in her group gasped, their eyes rounding. She couldn't blame them. He was pretty intimidating.

Artemis expected him to pass them by without speaking. But to her surprise, he stopped. *Yikes!* Right in front of *her*!

His piercing blue eyes practically bored holes right through her. "Aren't you the one in charge of the Games?" he demanded.

Her throat tightened a little. *Uh-oh.* Was there some trouble she didn't know about?

"Yes, sort of," she replied, her voice coming out as a squeak. How embarrassing! But who wouldn't be nervous to have the principal looming over them? Especially since he stood seven feet tall with bulging muscles! Not only was Zeus the MOA principal, he was also King of the Gods and Ruler of the Heavens. There was no one more powerful! Or fearsome.

"Here." Opening one of his big, beefy hands, he held out a long, ornate, silver key. "An order of supplies came this morning. Bags of pink sand. I had Hermes put them in the storage rooms in back of the gym. If any more supplies arrive, they'll be delivered there, too. You'll need this key to get in and out."

"Oh. Thanks." Artemis jumped as a tiny jolt of electricity passed through her when she took the key. Zeus's touch was electric—literally. He could fry you with a mere flick of his fingers if he wanted to.

In the corner of her brain she heard Persephone lead the rest of the tour group farther down the hall to look at the MOA trophy case while Artemis was busy with Zeus. Unfortunately, Apollo and Acteaon went along to explain some of the sports trophies and banners on display there. Penthe was sticking to Actaeon's side.

Zeus lifted an eyebrow at her. "Preparations going okay?"

"Preparations? Oh, you mean for the Games, right?" Artemis had a feeling he didn't really want to hear about all the problems. Like that the stuffed beanbag animals for the relay races hadn't been delivered yet. She would have preferred that the girls hand off traditional batons rather than stuffed animals. But she'd given in to her three best goddessgirl friends on that issue.

Besides checking on the beanbag order, she also needed to find out if the new targets had been delivered for the archery competitions. At least the extra pink sand she'd ordered for the long-jump pits had come. That was one thing she could check off her long to-do list.

Tap. Tap. Tap. The toe of one of Zeus's golden sandals tapped the shiny marble floor impatiently. "Well?" he prompted.

"Um. Yeah. Everything's going great."

"It better be." Zeus ran his fingers through his wild red hair and mumbled, "Because there's enough trouble headed our way. We don't need any more."

Artemis gulped. What did he mean by that? She knew he hadn't been in favor at first of the girls holding their own Olympic Games. She'd been the one to talk him into it. If one little thing went wrong, would he cancel them? Hurriedly, she forced a smile, saying, "You can count on me."

"Good—I will!" Zeus boomed out. Then he spun on his heel and continued down the hall toward his office. Over his shoulder, he called back, "And don't lose that key!"

She panicked for a second when she realized she was no longer holding it. But then she found it in the pocket of her chiton, where she'd automatically tucked it away. *Phew.* "Don't worry. I won't!" she called after him.

"Wow!" a girl said when Artemis rejoined the tour group by the trophy cases. "You are so brave." All the girls in the group were gazing at her in awe now. "I'd be scared to death to talk to him!" another girl added.

"It was no big deal," Artemis replied with a shrug. If you acted brave, people usually believed you were. She'd figured that out in Beast-ology class while facing off against some pretty terrifying creatures.

But she was feeling antsy to get that pink sand delivery sent to the long-jump pits. Should she go? Persephone could probably handle the rest of the tour on her own. Especially now that Actaeon and Apollo were helping.

Still, Artemis hated to leave Actaeon and Penthe here together. She glared at them, chatting away. This whole tour idea of Hera's was turning out to be a disaster, in her opinion.

The front doors opened behind them and another tour group entered the front hall. They were laughing. Obviously the girls in that group were enjoying *their* tour, she thought.

Aphrodite and Athena were leading it. Aphrodite was the goddessgirl of love and beauty and Athena was the brainiest girl at MOA. Together with Artemis and Persephone, the four goddessgirls were all best friends, and the most popular girls at the Academy.

Glancing up, Aphrodite caught Artemis's eye and winked. Her long golden hair glistened in a ray of sunlight that shone in through a high window. In honor of the Games, she'd threaded her hair with blue and gold ribbons—MOA's colors. The same double-G gold charm necklace that each of the four goddessgirl friends wore dangled at her throat.

Whatever funny thing Aphrodite had told her group to make them laugh, it couldn't have come from the official MOA tour guide scroll, Artemis decided. That thing was as dry as month-old ambrosia toast!

While Penthe continued to flirt with Actaeon, Apollo came over to Artemis. "Are you almost done?" he asked. "We should be at the range. I checked out some of the other archers, and you're going to have some stiff competition."

"Go ahead," said Persephone, overhearing. "I can finish the tour."

"You sure?" Artemis asked. She'd scoped out the other archers too. The two Egyptian goddessgirls had looked pretty good. But these Amazons, and one of the Norse goddessgirls, were going to be toughest to beat. Still, as much as she wanted to be off practicing, and as much as she needed to check up on game preparations, she also felt like she should see the tour through to the end.

"Yes! Go," said Persephone, making shooing motions with her pale hands.

"Okay. Thanks." Big-time relieved, Artemis let go of her guide scroll. It rolled itself shut in midair with a loud *snap*. "Go, scroll. Zoom! Up to my room!" she called out before it could hit the floor.

"Whoa!" a mortal girl in her group exclaimed.

Her eyes followed the scroll as it zoomed up the stairs, heading for the girls' dorm on the fourth floor. "That was amazing!"

Artemis grinned and bowed as several of the girls in her tour group applauded. She should've thought about using magic to liven things up before. To mortals, nothing was as fascinating as the magical feats immortals could perform!

Mortals that weren't Penthesilea, that is. She was still talking to Actaeon. Neither of them had even noticed when the guide scroll whooshed away. Well, worrying about that Amazon was a waste of time, Artemis decided.

There were other, more *important* things to worry about. Principal Zeus was counting on her. And so were the girls! To make sure that the Girl Games wouldn't end up as a one-time thing, she needed to make Zeus proud. And that meant everything had to go perfectly.

With her mind stuffed full of details she needed to take care of, Artemis took off, promising to meet Apollo for target practice later that afternoon.

2

Persephone

Thursday morning.

A HALF HOUR LATER THE TOUR WAS OVER
and Persephone was on her way to the sports fields.
There were lots of other students there already, practicing for the Games. Including Hades. But he was
waiting to *coach* her. In the long jump. Seeing her
coming, he waved, flashing her that sweet smile that

always lightened her heart. She waved back.

"Hey, Persephone," a girl who'd been in her group called out to her. "Good tour!"

"Thanks," she called back. She'd really enjoyed being a tour guide. After Artemis had left, she'd entertained the girls with stories about the teachers at MOA.

She told them about Mr. Cyclops, who taught Hero-ology and liked to go barefoot. Sometimes kids stole his gigantic sandals and hid them in odd places.

And when they'd walked past Principal Zeus's office and glimpsed his assistant, Ms. Hydra, Persephone had explained about her nine heads. How her green head was grumpy, her purple head was impatient, and so on.

"Tour go okay?" Hades asked as she came up to him.

Persephone nodded, watching him groom the sand in one of the pits with a wooden rake. "Mm-hm. Artemis had to leave early, so I took over at the end." She paused.

"This week has been crazy. We've spent time planning the Games, but we also have to find time to practice for them. We've all got a lot of responsibility right now. Especially Artemis. I can tell she's worried."

Hades leaned against the rake. "So is Apollo," he commented. "He says Artemis may be an expert archer, but other schools have sent their best archers to these Games too. He wants her to win!"

Since when had the boys started caring so much? Persephone wondered. Not long ago they hadn't even wanted the girls to have their own Games!

Getting down on his knees, Hades eyed the surface of the sand critically. Apollo might be anxious for Artemis to win the archery championship, but Hades seemed just as eager for Persephone to win the long jump. He cared about her chances way more than she did. She just wanted to have fun!

Hades' long dark hair fell over his face as he smoothed the sand. "This pink sand is so weird," he said, letting some of it sift through his fingers.

"So *girly,* you mean?" Persephone teased. "This is a *girls'* Olympics, you know. We can color the sand however we want!" Besides being pink, the sand was also magical. But its magic wouldn't give immortal jumpers any advantage over mortal jumpers. So they'd decided it was okay to use it despite the "no magic" rule Artemis had made for the Games.

Hades was grinning. "You're right," he agreed. "Pink is good." When she'd first met him, he'd rarely smiled. He'd been so moody all the time. He still was once in a while, and that appealed to one side of her—a darker side. But her bright side liked seeing him smile like this.

"Ready to get to work?"

She nodded. He wanted her to win, and she didn't

want to let him down. Still, it was a lot of pressure.

"Okay, then," Hades said. "Let's get cracking!" He went to stand near the take-off board in front of the pit. "You know the drill," he said.

Nodding, Persephone backed up a number of yards to give herself room for a running start. "Get into a rhythm as you approach the board," he reminded her. "Make your last three steps the fastest."

All around her in identical sand pits, other girls were practicing jumps too. Persephone shut them out of her mind, as Hades had coached her to do. He didn't want her comparing herself to them. He wanted her to concentrate on *her* jumps alone.

As she prepared to run, she tried to remember everything he'd taught her. There were four parts to a jump: 1) the approach to the board, 2) the takeoff after your foot hit the board, 3) the flight through the air, and 4) the landing. She closed her eyes for a few seconds and tried to picture herself doing them all perfectly. Then she opened her eyes again.

Okay. Go! she said under her breath. As she sprinted toward the take-off board, she was conscious of her arms and legs pumping rhythmically. So far, so good. As she hit the board, she kept her head up, looking ahead as Hades had trained her to do. A hard push-off and then she was sailing over the pit, cycling her arms and legs forward.

Thump! She on her rear in the pink sand. It magically swirled up from the pit high around her. It whirled into the air overhead and quickly formed the numbers fourteen and five. Then it all fell back into the pit again.

Seeing her score, Hades punched a fist in the air. "Fourteen feet, five inches! Awesome."

"Thanks," said Persephone. But she knew she'd have to hit at least sixteen feet in order to win. And to do that, she needed to land forward instead of backward. Every part of her jump needed to be just right.

"Try not to tense up as you land," Hades instructed as she stood and brushed the sand from her chiton. "When your heels hit, your knees need to give a little. That way your hips can move forward."

"Okay," she said. And she *would* try. She really would. But despite her best efforts, she wasn't sure she had what it took to be a championship jumper. In fact, it was kind of Artemis's fault that she had to do the long jump at all.

Artemis had made a rule that each participant in the Games had to enter at least two events—one team and one individual. If not for that rule, Persephone would've been happy just to compete as a member of

MOA's cheer team—the Goddessgirl Squad.

As she left the pit to get ready to practice her jump again, she wondered why Hades had such confidence in her abilities. Did she have more potential than she thought? Or was he only fooling himself?

3

Aphrodite

Thursday, early afternoon.

WHERE IS EVERYONE? APHRODITE WONDERED.

She was sitting alone at the four goddessgirls' usual

table in the cafeteria, waiting for her friends to show up

for lunch.

Suddenly, across from her, Artemis plunked down

her lunch tray. It hit the table so hard that Artemis's

silverware bounced up in the air. Her three dogs, who followed her almost everywhere, dove under the table to sniff around for random food crumbs.

"Everything okay?" Aphrodite asked, taking a sip of nectar.

"No." Artemis flopped into her chair. "Hermes' Delivery Service is behind schedule. So the new targets we ordered and those silly stuffed beanbag animals for the relays still aren't here yet."

Aphrodite jabbed her fork into her nectaroni. She was getting a little tired of Artemis's attitude. Sure, the girls-only Olympics had been Artemis's idea. But all the MOA girls had worked hard on them. These Olympic Games belonged to *all* the girls. And those "silly" beanbag animals—to be handed off in place of batons in the relay races—had been Aphrodite's idea.

Besides the relays, the girls at the Academy had

voted to include a two-hundred-meter footrace, long-jumping, thumb-wrestling, swimming, archery, and cheer in the Games. Seven events in all. It was a lot for a one-day Olympics, but some of the events would take place at the same time. Cheer was scheduled last.

The idea to include cheerleading had also been Aphrodite's. Of course, Artemis hadn't been thrilled about that, either. She'd only gone along with it because Persephone and Athena had suggested it might get more girls to join in the Games—which it had.

In fact, the cheer competition was shaping up to be the most popular event of the whole Olympics! And in Aphrodite's opinion, giving the events creative girly-twists like pink sand (her idea, too) was going to make them that much more fun. But try to convince Artemis of that!

"Don't worry so much," Aphrodite said mildly.

"Hermes will come through. There's still lots of time."

Artemis tore off three chunks of her hero sandwich and dropped them under the table for her dogs. "Not really. Just two days."

A brief scuffle broke out underneath the table, and one of the dogs knocked against Aphrodite's legs. "Ye gods," she said, scooting back her chair. "Couldn't they learn some table manners?" She didn't exactly dislike dogs, but they were so clumsy and . . . drooly!

"Sorry," said Artemis, hardly paying attention. "Hey," she said, changing the subject, "how are your footrace practices going?"

"Okay," Aphrodite said, just as Persephone and Athena finally showed up. All of them except Persephone were going to be in the two-hundred-meter footrace as one of their individual competitions.

Aphrodite had wanted to be in the relay race, too, so

she could hand off those "silly" stuffed animals. But the relays and cheer were both team events and she didn't have time to practice with two teams. So she'd decided on doing cheer with her friends.

"Is Ares a good coach?" Persephone asked, over-hearing.

"Mm-hm. He knows what he's doing. But he's a little intense when it comes to sports, especially running," Aphrodite admitted. Ares, her crush, was the fastest runner at MOA. He'd even won the footrace champion-ship in the boys' Olympics. Naturally he'd encouraged her to choose racing as her individual event.

"How about Hades?" she asked Persephone. "Is he a good coach too?"

Persephone nodded. "But he's a lot more into the whole competition thing than I am. Still, it's really nice of him to coach me. Especially since I'm new to jumping."

Aphrodite swirled her straw in her nectar. "I know what you mean about the competition thing. It's nice of the boys to help, but sometimes they push too hard. Maybe it's just because Ares is the god of war, but lately he's been treating me like a soldier he's training for battle!"

The others all laughed at that, and Aphrodite joined in. Still, she wondered if Persephone worried about letting down Hades as much as *she* worried about disappointing Ares. She'd *like* to run faster—as Ares kept urging her. But she hated to break a sweat. As the goddessgirl of beauty, it was so un-*her*!

Just then, from the corner of her eye, Aphrodite noticed a beautiful, fair-skinned goddessgirl in a feathered cloak. She had blue eyes and blond-gold hair. Just like Aphrodite. But the most striking thing about her was the fabulous gold necklace she wore, which was studded with dazzling jewels.

"Wow. Look at her," she whispered to her friends.

Artemis glanced over one shoulder. "That's Freya," she said, waving to the girl, who waved back. "She's one of the Norse goddesses. I met her at target shooting practice with her friend Skadi. They're good—at archery, I mean."

"How about her?" Aphrodite asked, nodding toward another goddessgirl who walked by right then. The girl's red robe sparkled with jewels. A flat-topped hat with beads hanging from its brim partly covered her glossy black hair. "I love her robe, and her hat is fantastic."

"Her name's Mazu," Persephone told the others. "She was in Medusa and Pandora's tour group this morning, with another girl called Wen Shi. Pandora told me they're swimmers from China. And get this: Wen Shi brought five pet baby snakes with her."

"Oh!" said Artemis, looking at Persephone. "Wen Shi must have been that girl we saw on the tour this morning. The one who didn't back away from Medusa's snaky hair."

"Makes sense," said Aphrodite, grinning.

As she, Persephone, and Artemis traded more stories about the athletes they'd met, Aphrodite realized that Athena wasn't saying a word. Her head was bent forward so that her long, wavy brown hair hid most of her face as she quietly ate her bowl of yambrosia stew.

Was something the matter? Relationship problems, perhaps? Aphrodite had a knack for sniffing out that sort of distress. As the goddessgirl of love, such matters were of deep concern to her!

Come to think of it, she hadn't seen Athena's crush, Heracles, for a couple of days. And a quick glance around showed that he wasn't in the cafeteria. Since he always wore a lion-skin cape, whose jaws fit around his head like a helmet, he was hard to miss!

Leaning toward Athena, Aphrodite said casually, "I haven't seen Heracles in a while. What's up with him?"

Immediately Athena set down her fork. "He and the rest of the wrestling team went to a meet in North Africa to compete with some giants. He's not sure they'll be back in time to see our Games."

"Oh, no," Aphrodite said sympathetically. No wonder Athena seemed sad. "Hey," she said in an attempt to cheer her up, "Want to go to the Immortal Marketplace with me after lunch? I'm going to look for a cute new running outfit for Saturday."

Athena smiled but shook her head. "Can't. I need to do some practice sprints to prepare for the footrace. And I really should start studying for next week's Hero-ology quiz."

"Okay, but you're missing out," Aphrodite said. "Shopping is tons more fun than studying!" It had never made sense to her that Athena—the best student among them—would study for a quiz that was days away.

On the other hand, maybe if *she* spent as much time studying as Athena did, she'd make top grades too. Only, shopping was so much more enjoyable than studying, especially when you did it with friends. But when Persephone and Artemis also said they were too busy, Aphrodite decided to go shopping alone.

After lunch she grabbed a pair of winged sandals from the big basket beside MOA's bronze front doors. Slipping off her regular sandals, she parked them by the basket. And as soon as she was outside, she put on the winged ones.

Instantly the sandals' straps twined around her ankles and the silver wings at her heels began to flap.

Whoosh! The sandals zipped her across the courtyard at ten times normal walking speed. With her feet just inches above the ground, she descended Mount Olympus, skimming past boulders and trees.

In no time at all she reached the Marketplace, which was halfway between Earth and MOA. After skidding to a stop at the entrance, she untied her sandals. Then she looped the straps over the silver wings to hold them still so she could walk in the sandals instead of fly.

The market was huge and dazzling, with a high-ceilinged crystal roof. Its various shops, separated by row upon row of elegant columns, sold everything a god or goddess could possibly desire. Persephone's mom had a flower shop here called Demeter's Daisies, Daffodils, and Floral Delights.

And Hera ran a wedding shop called Hera's Happy Endings. Even though her shop kept her crazy busy,

Hera had promised to be at their Games on Saturday to hand out prizes.

The visitors at MOA had given Aphrodite lots of fashion ideas she was eager to try out, but she didn't have time to window shop today. She was on a mission. Her goal: to find the cutest running outfit ever!

After some searching, she found the perfect one at Cynisca's Spartan Sportswear. A cute, short, sparkly pink chiton that came with a pair of cropped matching leggings. It was *mega-dorable*!

On her way out of the Marketplace with her new purchase, Aphrodite passed through an atrium. At its center was a myrrh tree surrounded by a garden full of fragrant flowers.

"Mew, Mew."

Hearing the sad mewling sound, Aphrodite stopped in her tracks, startled.

"Mew, Mew." There it was again! It was coming from that garden. Setting her bag down, she searched among the flowers for the source of the sound.

And then she found it. It was a kitten! But not just any kitten. It was the cutest kitten she'd ever seen. It had sleek black fur, a white bib, and little white feet.

"Come here, sweetie. Are you hungry?" Aphrodite bent and reached out, wiggling her fingers in invitation.

"Mew, Mew." After a moment's hesitation, the kitten scampered toward her. It began purring the instant she picked it up.

Gazing into the kitten's beautiful, wistful green eyes, Aphrodite's heart melted. And she fell instantly, completely, and totally in love.

4

Athena

Thursday, midafternoon.

WHAT ARE YOU GOING TO DO WITH IT?"
Athena asked, staring doubtfully at the kitten. All four
goddessgirl friends had gathered in Aphrodite's room
to ooh and ahh over her newfound pet.

"It's a *him*," said Artemis, who knew the most about
animals. "A boy kitten."

Cuddling the kitten to her chest, Aphrodite answered Athena's question, sounding just a little defensive. "I'm going to keep him, of course. Poor baby. He was *abandoned.*"

"How awful," said Persephone, lightly rubbing the kitten's head. "He's *sooo* sweet. Who would do such a mean thing?"

"The shopkeepers around the atrium where I found him told me he'd been hanging around for days, looking hungry and lost," Aphrodite told them. "They put up signs, but no one claimed him."

Athena thought it was nice that the kitten had been rescued. But she had been hoping they could talk about their cheer routine for the Games.

The routine was one they'd done many times before and knew by heart. It was great. She just wasn't sure it would be strong enough to win against the amazing cheer teams they'd be competing against.

Maybe it was only that she was used to their old finale—the one where they magically sprouted wings and rose into the air holding hands. They'd had to change that part, though. To make things fair to the mortal athletes who couldn't use magic.

So now their routine just ended with them holding hands while doing the splits. It was an okay ending, but not spectacular. If they brainstormed ideas, maybe they could come up with something new. But everyone was too busy being excited about the kitten for that right now.

Artemis reached out to pet it. "What are you going to name him?" she asked Aphrodite. "How about Mark, since you got him at the *Mark*etplace?"

"Well, I was thinking about the name Myrrh, since I found him under a myrrh tree. And myrrh rhymes with purr," Aphrodite said thoughtfully. "But that sounds like a girl's name. So I think maybe I'll name him Adonis. Like in the philosopher Ovid's stories we studied in Literature-ology class."

"Adonis," Persephone repeated softly. She stuck a fingertip close to the kitten's face and its pink tongue darted out, licking her. "I *love* that name."

Athena sat on Aphrodite's spare bed. Most students shared a dorm room, like she and Pandora did. But though Aphrodite and Artemis had originally been roommates, Aphrodite had been a little icked out by sharing space with three dogs. So Artemis and her pooches had moved to an empty room next door.

Brushing her hand over the bed's plush red velvet comforter, which was stitched with a pattern of little white hearts, Athena wondered what the kitten's claws might do to Aphrodite's practically perfect room. But that wasn't the biggest problem with this kitten.

She broke the bad news in the kindest way she could. "It might be a good idea to check with my dad about keeping him. Before you get too attached."

Aphrodite and Persephone both looked at her in alarm. "Zeus? But what about his no-pets rule? What if he says no?" asked Aphrodite.

Persephone nodded. "Yeah. She can't take that chance!"

"Principal Zeus might make an exception for Adonis," Artemis said. "After all, he let me keep my dogs. And the deer that draw my carriage are allowed to roam the school grounds." She paused. "And he let Orion keep his dog when he came here as a foreign exchange student. Of course, that was only for a few days."

Aphrodite shook her head, her long golden hair

swaying. "Not good enough. Zeus hasn't let anyone else at MOA get a new pet for ages. Like Persephone said, I can't take the chance he might say no. I'm too in love with this little cutie!" She enfolded the kitten in both hands and touched the tip of her nose to his tiny pink one.

Athena picked up one of Aphrodite's puffy, heart-shaped pillows and hugged it to her chest. "So, what are you going to do then? Hide him?"

"Maybe," Aphrodite said.

Athena frowned. "Bad idea. If my dad finds out—"

"He won't!" Aphrodite interrupted firmly.

Artemis had emptied her quiver onto Aphrodite's desk and was sitting on her chair, checking her arrow tips for sharpness. "Athena's right," she told Aphrodite without looking up. "I know Ares is training you to be a fast runner. But are you fast enough to dodge Zeus's thunderbolts?"

"Ha, ha!" said Aphrodite. Reaching out, she grabbed a pillow from one of her beds and flung it at Artemis teasingly. Then she hugged Adonis close again, stroking the soft white fur on his neck. Glancing sideways at Athena, she said, "You won't rat me out to Zeus, will you?"

Athena snorted. "No way! What kind of friend do you think I am?"

"A good one," Aphrodite said quickly.

"The best," Persephone said, nodding in agreement.

"Doesn't mean I'm not worried," Athena added. "A secret this big won't be easy to keep."

Aphrodite held up Adonis and grinned. Pretending to be the kitten speaking, she said in a high voice, "I'm not that big. I'll be easy to hide."

"Just don't let Pheme find out," Artemis warned. "She can't keep a secret, even when she wants to!"

Pheme was the goddessgirl of gossip and rumor.

"I know, I know," said Aphrodite. She set the kitten down on the rug in front of a small bowl of milk. "Don't be such worrywarts. It'll all work out. It has to!"

"Be practical," Athena pressed. "Who'll take care of him while you're practicing for the Games?"

"Me," Persephone volunteered in a hurry. "I'll be sleeping over in Aphrodite's room for the next few nights, remember? Until the Games end." Ordinarily, Persephone lived at home with her mom.

Athena shrugged. "I guess that's a plan." But what about after the Games ended? she wondered silently. Aphrodite was a great friend, but she wasn't the best at thinking things through sometimes.

Gathering up her arrows, Artemis stood and announced that she had to meet Apollo for archery practice. When she also mentioned she was going to check the gym to see if Hermes had made any deliveries, Athena stood too. "I'll do it. You go on to practice." As she halfway expected, though, Artemis refused her help, saying, "That's okay. Zeus gave me the key. I'd better go."

Whatever! thought Athena, shrugging. When it came to the Games, it was like Artemis had forgotten how to trust anyone else to do anything to help out!

Aphrodite and Persephone were still cooing over the kitten when Artemis left. So Athena headed off too, going to her room to study.

The minute she opened the door to her dorm room, she spotted her roommate, Pandora, sitting in the middle of her bed. With her hands held out in front of her, she moved her thumbs up and down and side to side, then around in circles. Athena shot her a questioning glance.

"I'm practicing," Pandora explained. "I entered the thumb-wrestling competition, remember?"

Athena gave her a thumbs-up. "Awesome."

Pandora grinned. "How about you? How's practice going for your race?"

Athena checked the floor under their window to see if a breeze had delivered any messages from Heracles. Sadly, there was nothing.

"Okay, I guess," she told Pandora as she sat down at her desk and reached for her red Hero-ology textscroll. "Although I'd feel better about my chances in a contest of wits. Something like Apollo's match against that Python riddler in the boys' Olympics. But then again, if I actually *had* any wits, I guess I would've suggested such a contest for our Games back when the events list was still being decided!"

"You'll do okay?" said Pandora, who was doing little

thumb push-ups against the wall now. Even when she said things that should end with a period, she couldn't help making them sound like questions.

Athena wasn't really sure. Everyone else was practicing so hard. And getting good coaching besides. Since so many girls had signed up for the footraces, there was going to be a round of preliminary elimination races on Friday.

If she lost out in the elims, she might not even make it to the actual championship race in the Olympic Games on Saturday. She wasn't sure she was good enough to qualify, and it was making her anxious. She knew she shouldn't feel this way, but she only liked to do things she was good at.

Well, there was *one* thing she was definitely good at. Studying. It relaxed her. Maybe too much. Because after a few minutes of it, she was feeling sort of tired.

She laid her head on her desk for just a minute.

A half hour later, she woke up with a kink in her neck.

What a strange dream she'd been having, she thought as she turned her head side to side to work out the kink. Now that the dream was starting to fade, however, she could only remember snatches of it.

It had been something about Pegasus—the winged horse Zeus had gotten as a wedding present to carry his thunderbolts when he went sky-riding. There'd been a black-haired boy in her dream, too, riding the horse. *Heracles, maybe?* She hadn't seen his face. But he had black hair. And it made sense she'd dream about him since she was missing him.

There'd also been a magnificent and magical golden bridle for the horse in her dream. Of that part she was sure, because she could still see it in her mind. She could even picture herself casting the spell that created it. Weird!

But what had happened after that was a mystery. Before it ended, her dream had drifted away like smoke in the aftermath of one of her dad's infamous lightning-bolt strikes. *Pfft!*

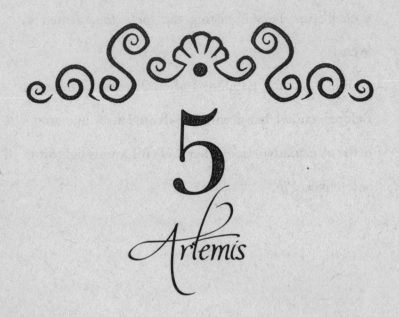

5

Artemis

Thursday, late afternoon.

COME ON, GUYS!" ARTEMIS CALLED TO HER dogs. She held her dorm room door open, letting them dash into the hall. She'd left them cooped up while she was next door at Aphrodite's, afraid they might chase the kitten. So now the three of them—Suez, her bloodhound; Amby, her beagle; and Nectar, her greyhound—

were full of energy. They romped happily around her as she went to meet Apollo at the archery range.

That new kitten was pretty sweet, she mused, as she crossed the courtyard and started downhill to the sports fields. But she hoped Aphrodite wouldn't wait too long before asking Principal Zeus if she could keep him.

Like Athena, she didn't think little Adonis was going to be all that easy to hide. Sooner or later someone would hear him meowing. Or he'd escape from Aphrodite's room somehow. Kittens were curious and always getting into mischief.

She broke into a run and her dogs went wild with joy, loping after her. Though she had a special affection for all animals, dogs were her forever favorite.

Since the archery field was behind the gymnasium, she cut past the delivery entrance at the side of the gym. There was a beautiful silver chariot with mighty white wings parked near the doors. The Hermes' Delivery Service chariot! A god in a winged cap—Hermes himself—was busily lifting boxes out of the back of the chariot.

"Are those what I think they are?" she called out. Hermes sent her a thumbs-up.

"Good!" she called to him. "Let me help." She hurried over to unlock the storage room door with the silver key Zeus had given her. After the storage room was open, she and Hermes began carrying in the boxes, which he'd stacked on the ground next to his chariot.

There were more boxes than she'd thought there would be, but what a relief that the targets and stuffed animals had arrived at last. One less thing to worry about. Everything would still need to be unpacked before Saturday's competitions, though. She'd do it herself, just to be sure everything was as it should be.

"So much to do, so little time," she murmured. After Hermes left, she patted the pocket of her chiton and felt the hard edge of the key inside. *Phew.* She hadn't lost it. She'd need it to get at the boxes again later.

When she reached the range, she spotted Apollo. He was sitting in the stands, watching the Amazons practice. When he saw her, he climbed down. "You're late," he said, frowning.

"I stopped to help Hermes unload some Game supplies," Artemis explained. Her dogs leaped around her brother, overjoyed to see him.

Apollo grunted. "Well, I can't stay long."

"Why not?" Artemis asked.

"Something else I need to do," Apollo mumbled. Before she could ask him what that was, he said, "Show me your arrows."

She dumped them out of her quiver. As he inspected

them closely, checking to see how well she'd sharpened them, she glanced toward the Amazons. Four of them had lined up together. In perfect synchrony they fired off a volley of arrows.

Zzing! Zzing! Zzing! Zzing! All four arrows struck the bull's-eye. Amazons had a reputation as fierce warriors, and Artemis had to admire their skill. When they turned to nock another round of arrows, she recognized two of them—Penthe and Hippolyta.

"They're good," she said, hearing the envy in her voice. They were going to be tough competition for sure!

"No they aren't."

"Huh?" Artemis glanced at Apollo and realized he was talking about her arrow tips. Dissatisfied with the job she'd done, he pulled a sharpening stone from the pocket of his tunic and went to work on them.

"Artemis!" a voice called out to her. Her face lit

up. *Actaeon!* As he came toward her, her dogs ran to greet him. Suez reached him first. Leaping up, the bloodhound planted his front paws in the middle of Actaeon's chest and proceeded to lick his face.

"Down, boy!" Artemis called out, rushing over. But Suez was too excited to obey.

"It's okay," said Actaeon. He ruffled the fur on the hound's neck and then stooped to pet Nectar and Amby, too. She was glad her dogs liked him. They were good judges of character.

Finally, Actaeon straightened. Brushing his light-brown hair away from his face, he smiled at her. "I came to help with your practice. What can I do?"

You could act like you like me in front of those dumb Amazons, she wanted to say. But all she said was, "Could you maybe watch my dogs while I shoot?"

"Sure," he said.

As he rounded the dogs up and herded them toward the stands, Artemis allowed herself to imagine that she'd actually said what she'd been thinking. And that he'd given her the same response as he had to her actual question.

In your dreams, she chided herself. Goopy stuff like that was for girls like Aphrodite. Actaeon considered Artemis a girl pal. They'd held hands together exactly three times, and it had been a while since the last time.

It was a few seconds before she noticed that Apollo had finished sharpening her arrows and was holding them out to her. "I know you're goddess of the moon as well as the hunt," he said. "But do you think you could stop mooning over Actaeon long enough to practice now?"

"Shut up!" Artemis whispered, elbowing him. She glanced worriedly toward Actaeon, hoping he hadn't heard. He was too far away, but *still*. Apollo should know better.

Snatching the arrows, she slipped them into her quiver. Apollo just grinned. She wished he'd stop teasing her for having a crush. Maybe he'd stop if he knew how much it bothered her. Or, knowing him, he'd probably just do it more!

She spotted a free target over by the Amazons, and started toward it. But just as she reached the firing line, Penthe spoke up in a snotty voice, "Cute outfit today, Artemis."

"Yeah," agreed Hippolyta. Then both girls put their heads together and giggled.

Artemis looked down at her red chiton. It was wrinkled and there was a little tear near the hem. She never paid much attention to fashion, but now she put her hand over the rip to hide it. Although they'd embarrassed her, she made herself pretend they hadn't. Straightening, she forced a smile. "Hey, thanks for the compliment!" she called out to them.

Penthe just narrowed her eyes. Her silver bracelets jangled as she smoothed her dress. It was a violet-colored *peplos* with gold, leaf-shaped clasps at each shoulder. She looked pretty. Had Actaeon noticed?

Before Artemis could look over at him to check, two Egyptian goddessgirls walked by carrying archery bows. Their kohl-lined eyes were exotic looking, and they wore tall crowns that made them appear to be almost as tall as the Amazons.

"You're Artemis, right?" one of them asked. When Artemis nodded, the girl flashed a smile. "Want to come shoot with us?" she asked. Her crown was bright red, and it had a curly wire poking out of it that resembled the proboscis of a bee.

"There are three free targets down at the end," the other Egyptian goddess added. Antelope horns stuck out from either side of her crown. "I'm Neith, by the way. Satet and I are huge fans of yours. We thought we could get some tips by watching you shoot."

"Okay. Sure," said Artemis. Feeling flattered, she turned to go with them.

Penthe's eyes bugged out at them. "Are you all crazy? You're competitors! You shouldn't help each other. Sharing your shooting secrets is a big mistake, if you ask me."

Hippolyta smacked her gum, looking back and forth between the Egyptian goddesses and Artemis. "Yeah. Don't you want to win?"

"Yes, but we also believe in good sportsmanship," said Satet.

Artemis nodded. "The Girl Games are supposed to

be about cultural exchange. That means sharing. We'll all get better at our sports if we learn from one another."

Suddenly Penthe looked worried and a little jealous, like maybe she wanted to change her mind and share tips too. But the Egyptian girls had already linked arms on either side of Artemis and begun to lead her away.

As they headed for some targets at the end of the row, Artemis told them, "Thanks for—" She paused, unsure of how to finish what she'd started to say. *Thanks for rescuing me?* She wasn't even sure Satet and Neith had *known* that the Amazons were picking on her before they'd come over.

Neith rolled her eyes. "Those Amazons are all about winning. They need to be taken down a notch."

"Besides, we're serious," Satet added. "We really do want to learn from you. So show us your stuff."

Artemis grinned. "All right. If you say so." When

they reached the shooting line, she pulled a silver arrow from her quiver. She fitted the notched end into her bowstring. Pulling back on the string, she took careful aim at the target. Then she released her arrow.

Zzzing! It shot toward the center of the bull's-eye. *Not bad,* she thought as she watched it find its mark. But having seen some of the other archers—especially the Amazons and the Norse archer, Skadi—she knew she would have to shoot perfectly *every single time* to have a chance at winning Saturday's competition.

6

Persephone

Thursday night.

PERSEPHONE SAT ON THE FLOOR OF APHRODITE'S
room and dangled a pomegranate-red hair ribbon
in front of Adonis. She giggled as the kitten leaped at
it, batting it with his white-booted paws. She'd found
the ribbon in Aphrodite's drawer. That girl had so
many ribbons that Persephone figured she surely

wouldn't care if Adonis scratched this one up.

She hoped Hades wasn't mad at her for blowing off their afternoon practice session. He'd looked kind of mad, though, when she'd told him she wanted to take a nap instead. Even though she'd tried to act sleepy and yawned a lot, she wasn't sure he'd bought her performance. He could usually see through her lies like no one else.

She would've liked to tell him about Adonis, but she and her friends had all agreed to keep the kitten a secret—even from their crushes. The fewer people who knew about the kitten, the better.

It was more fun playing with Adonis than practicing her jumps anyway. He was so cute with his pink nose, his curious green eyes, and his soft black-and-white fur. She was falling in love with him every bit as much as Aphrodite was!

"Are you hungry, sweetie?" Persephone asked when Adonis grew tired of playing. "I'll get you some snacks." Since there was no kitten food around, she sneaked into Artemis's room next door and snagged a few of her dog treats. Then she crumbled them into pieces. While the kitten gobbled those down, she found a cup in the bathroom down the hall and got him some water, too.

Adonis was so dainty, the way he picked up the crumbs one at a time and crunched them down, then lapped up the water with his little pink tongue. It was fun taking care of him like this. Almost like he was her own.

After he was full, he curled up on Persephone's lap and fell asleep. He was still napping there as she sat cross-legged on Aphrodite's spare bed—*her* bed for the weekend—when Aphrodite returned. As she burst in the door, Persephone set aside the *Teen Scrollazine* she'd been reading.

"Adonis!" Aphrodite exclaimed. "I missed you, cutie-pie!" She practically dove for the kitten, snatching him from Persephone's lap.

A startled "mew!" escaped the kitten. Surprised and maybe a little scared, he accidentally knocked the scrollazine on the floor and almost scratched Persephone's leg. Aphrodite held him up in front of her face. His back legs dangled and squirmed in midair as she kissed the top of his head. "Did you miss me too?" she cooed.

No. He didn't, Persephone felt like saying. Instead, she said huffily, "You need to support his feet."

"I *know* how to hold a kitten," Aphrodite said with a trace of irritation. Still, she shifted her arms to better support him.

Then her eyes widened. "Godsamighty!" she squeaked in alarm. "He's going to the bathroom!" She quickly set him on Persephone's *Teen Scrollazine* on the floor. A puddle formed around him on the parchment.

"It's not his fault!" said Persephone. "He needs a cat box. With cat litter in it."

"Well, I haven't had time," said Aphrodite as the two girls cleaned up the soggy scrollazine. Afterward they bundled Adonis in a towel and sneaked him outside just in case he still had to *go*.

As he scratched in the dirt, they kept a lookout. Luckily, by now most everyone was at dinner and the coast was clear. "He's going to need some proper kitten food," Aphrodite said.

Persephone had to bite her tongue to keep from saying that she should've thought of that earlier. But really, if things had been left up to Aphrodite, Adonis would've starved by now! "I fed him some dog treats from Artemis's room while you were gone. And I gave him water too."

"*Dog* treats?" A horrified expression came over Aphrodite's face. "Those can't be good for him!"

Yikes, thought Persephone. From Aphrodite's reaction, you'd think she'd tried to poison Adonis! "They won't kill him," she said stiffly. "But if you're going to the Supernatural Market, don't forget cat litter, too. Want me to watch him while you go shopping?"

Now that the kitten had done his business, Aphrodite wrapped him up in the towel again, leaving an opening for air to get in. "No, I think I'll take him with me. So he can try some of the different chow they sell. So I don't buy something he doesn't like."

"Uh-huh." Persephone had a feeling the real reason

was that Aphrodite didn't want to leave her alone with the kitten again. Since neither girl was willing to leave Adonis with the other, they both decided to go.

The market was beyond the sports fields. To avoid anyone who might be out practicing late, they skirted the fields by a wide margin. They didn't want anyone asking questions about the bundle Aphrodite was carrying.

When they were almost to the market, Persephone elbowed Aphrodite's arm. "Uh-oh. Pheme alert," she whispered, nodding toward the orange-haired girl just leaving the store. She was carrying an issue of *Teen Scrollazine* that she'd probably just bought. Pheme always made sure to get the newest scrollazines, so she could learn the best bits of celebrity gossip before anyone else.

"Oh, great," said Aphrodite. "The nosiest girl in the whole Academy!"

Before they could hide, Pheme spotted them. "Yoo-hoo!" she called out. "What're you up to?" As usual, her words puffed from her lips to form little cloud letters above her head.

"Nothing much," said Persephone, trying to sound as if that were true. In fact, her heart was beating faster than the wings on a pair of magic flying sandals.

Pheme's eyes, which rarely missed anything, went straight to the lumpy towel Aphrodite was holding. "Whatcha got there?" she asked.

"You mean this old towel?" said Aphrodite, as if she hadn't even realized she was holding it. "I just . . . um . . . found it. Somebody must've dropped it. Probably one of the girls practicing for the swimming event."

"I'm going past the laundry on my way back to MOA. Want me to drop it off?" Pheme reached for the towel.

Aphrodite twisted away from her in alarm. "Don't touch it!" she yelled.

Startled, Pheme drew back. "Okay, okay. I won't."

The towel started wiggling. "Mew, Mew."

"Achoo! Achoo!" Persephone fake-sneezed to cover the kitten's meows. "Allergies," she explained. Taking Aphrodite's arm, she steered her toward the market's door. "That's why we're here," she called back over her shoulder to Pheme. "To get some herbal medicine. See you later!"

Giving the two of them a puzzled look, Pheme then shrugged and started back toward the Academy.

"Phew," said Aphrodite, giggling. "That was close."

"No kidding," Persephone agreed, joining her laughter. Inside the Supernatural Market the girls bought some kitten chow and kitty litter. Since they hadn't had dinner, they also got some snacks to share on the way home. Then they hurried outside again.

They'd worried that Pheme might change her mind and decide to wait for them, but when they came out, she was nowhere in sight. "Do you think she'll forget about the towel incident?" Aphrodite asked anxiously as they started back to the Academy.

Persephone couldn't help smiling at her choice of words. Aphrodite liked to call any troublesome event an "incident," even something as serious as the Trojan War! Which Aphrodite had accidently helped start. Fortunately, they made it back to the dorm room without further "incidents."

Persephone had hoped Aphrodite would offer to let her carry Adonis part of the way, but she didn't. And when the girls crawled into bed to sleep, Aphrodite tucked Adonis in with her.

In the middle of the night Persephone woke to the

sound of the kitten's meows. She sat up. He was sitting on the floor. Somehow he'd managed to tumble out of Aphrodite's bed. Persephone slid out of her bed and picked him up.

"Huh? Wha?" Aphrodite mumbled.

"Shh," Persephone whispered. "Go back to sleep." She was relieved when Aphrodite rolled over and did just that.

"Sweet Adonis," Persephone cooed, as she tucked the kitten in with her. "You can sleep with me. *I'll* take care of you."

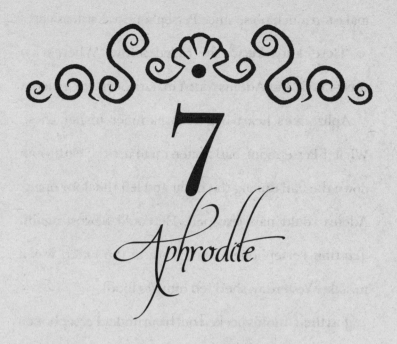

7

Aphrodite

Friday morning.

WHEN APHRODITE WOKE THE NEXT MORN-
ing, she looked for Adonis under her red-velvet comforter. He wasn't there! Or on the floor, either. Was he
hiding somewhere?

She hopped out of bed and hunted for him, opening
drawers and digging through her closet. She tried not to

make too much noise since Persephone was still asleep.

"Here, kitty, kitty," she called softly. "Where's my sweet kitty?" But Adonis didn't make a peep. Or a meow.

Aphrodite's heart began to hammer in her chest. What if Persephone had gotten up to use the bathroom down the hall during the night and left the door open? Adonis could have escaped. He could be lost again! Trusting Persephone to take care of the kitten was a mistake. Yesterday, she'd fed him *dog* food!

Just then Adonis peeked out from under Persephone's covers, looking sleepy. "So there you are!" Aphrodite whispered. Relief flooded through her as she scooped up the kitten. Making sure she supported his back feet this time, she cuddled him to her chest.

"How did you end up in Persephone's bed?" she asked him, though she could guess the answer. It was obvious, wasn't it? Persephone had waited until

Aphrodite had fallen asleep, and then she'd *stolen* Adonis.

Well, if Persephone wants a kitten, she should get her own, thought Aphrodite. *Because* I *found Adonis yesterday, so he belongs to* me*!*

While Persephone went on sleeping, Aphrodite poured some kitten chow into a small saucer for Adonis. Then she sneaked down the hall to the bathroom and refilled his water bowl. She nearly spilled it when she turned from the sink, however. Because Pandora was standing in the doorway!

"Uh, Persephone gave me a plant," Aphrodite blurted out, in case the girl was wondering about the bowl. "It looked a little dry, so I thought I'd better water it." Since Persephone, like her mom, took a special interest in flowers and plants, Aphrodite's made-up story wasn't all that farfetched.

"Huh?" Pandora mumbled as she ran a hand through her tousled hair. Her bangs immediately snapped back into the shape of question marks on her forehead. Then she yawned and shuffled toward one of the stalls.

Phew! Close one, thought Aphrodite. When she got back to her room, she set down the bowl of water, and Adonis lapped some up. While she was watching him, Aphrodite's stomach growled, reminding her that she hadn't eaten a real dinner last night.

She got dressed, then glanced over at Persephone. Should she wake her? They could take turns going to the cafeteria and watching Adonis. No. She didn't want to leave Adonis with Persephone. That girl was getting too possessive of the kitten for her own good—too possessive for Aphrodite's good, anyway!

Besides, Adonis was getting the same look on his face as he'd had last night, right before he'd made a puddle on her scrollazine. *Ye gods!* She'd forgotten to get a box for the cat litter she'd bought last night.

"Wait! I'll take you outside," she told the kitten, crossing her fingers that they'd make it before there was another accident.

Wrapping him in a towel hadn't been such a great idea, so she reached in the back of her closet and grabbed the first thing she found that might work as a carrier. It was a huge woven bag that she'd forgotten she even had. She halfway recalled buying it on impulse months ago, but she'd never used it, for some reason.

Quickly, Aphrodite stuffed a pink, heart-shaped bed pillow into the bottom of the bag to make it nice and comfy. As she gently set Adonis inside, Persephone snuffled and rolled over, but she didn't wake up. The kitten mewed softly and then curled up on top of the pillow.

Holding the bag, Aphrodite hurried down the hall and then took the marble staircase, checking on the kitten every few steps. Once outside the Academy, she ducked down a trail and let the kitten out. Just in time! As the kitten did his business, she studied the bag she'd brought him in.

Hmm. She didn't remember the floppy poppy-flower decoration on the front being quite so enormous. Or quite so bright yellow. But the bag was big and its weave was loose. Plenty of air would reach Adonis as she carried him inside. The bag made an excellent kitten carrier, she decided.

When Adonis was ready, he went back in the bag and curled up on the pink pillow again. "Good boy," Aphrodite told him. She carried him back up the trail, crossed the courtyard, and was soon inside the Academy again.

Aphrodite glanced toward the cafeteria. She was starving. It seemed dumb to go all the way upstairs to her room just to put Adonis inside. Besides, then Persephone would probably tuck him into her bed again.

"Try to be as still as a mouse," she whispered to Adonis as she pushed through the cafeteria door.

The cafeteria was packed with MOA students and some of the girls who were visiting. The sounds of their chatter and laughter filled her ears. All that noise combined with the banging of trays and the clatter of silverware would surely drown out any sounds Adonis might make, she decided. Seeing Athena already at their usual table, she headed there.

Athena's eyes rounded at the sight of the bright, floppy poppy bag Aphrodite set on the table. "Hi. Um. Nice bag," she said doubtfully.

Aphrodite nodded. "Yeah. It's *purr*-fect, don't you think? *Mew*-velous, in fact."

Athena's puzzled look suddenly changed to one of understanding. "Oh no!" she exclaimed. "You brought *him* here? Are you crazy?"

"No, just hungry. And we were out for his bathroom break, so . . ."

"Can he breathe in there?" Athena whispered.

"He's fine. Will you keep an eye on him while I grab something to eat, though?" She slid the bag in front of Athena. Athena nodded, clutching the bag and glancing nervously around as if she expected someone to try to peek inside it at any moment.

As Aphrodite got a tray and went to wait in the breakfast line, Ares left his table and ambled over to her. "Hey," he said, coming up behind her. Pushing a lock of her shiny golden hair behind one ear, she smiled up at him. Then she craned her neck to see the breakfast choices. *Hmm. Should I have oatmeal with nectar or ambrosia cakes or . . . ?*

"Up for one last practice before the eliminations this afternoon?" Ares asked.

"Um, no, I'm good," she told him, only half-listening. She was so preoccupied with thoughts of food and kittens that for once she hardly noticed how handsome he was, how tall and how blond.

In fact, now that she had Adonis, she wasn't quite so interested in the race, either. Oh, she still planned to do her best, but she wanted to spend as much time with her kitten as possible. Especially since she wanted him to bond with *her*, not Persephone!

"You may be 'good,' but you could be *better* with

more practice," Ares joked. "And we want you to ace today's elims and actually make it to the Olympics on Saturday, right?" He held up a hand to knuckle-bump her shoulder, but just then she reached for a plate of hambrosia and eggs that the eight-armed lunch lady held out, and he missed.

"Yeah, I guess." Aphrodite slid the plate onto her tray just as Artemis walked into the cafeteria with her three dogs right behind her. Immediately the hounds perked up and bounded toward the girls' table. *Ye gods!* Had they smelled Adonis?

"Well, how about if we just hang out? We can talk about the fine points of the perfect stride." Ares was saying. "Maybe—"

"Sorry, gotta run," Aphrodite told him in a rush. "Later."

He sent her a puzzled frown as she clutched her tray and dashed off. She would've liked to explain about the kitten. But she and her friends had agreed to keep him a secret. And, anyway, there was no time. She needed to rescue Adonis from those big, drooly kitten-sniffing dogs!

8

Athena

Friday morning.

ATHENA WAS HUGGING THE UGLY BAG AND
peeking inside now and then to check on the kitten
when Artemis's dogs raced over. They skidded to a stop
in front of her table and immediately began to push
their noses at the bag.

"Shoo!" Athena hissed, shoving them back. "Get

away!" But the dogs wouldn't budge. In fact, they just became even more kitten crazed. The beagle began to bay at the bag. "Aroo!"

Noisy conversations and the clatter of dishes weren't enough to drown that out! Students all around her began to turn toward the goddessgirls' table. Everyone was staring. The dogs jumped up and down in excitement, jostling her from every angle.

Ten minutes ago she'd been minding her own business, eating oatmeal and nectar. How had she gotten into this mess?

"Down, boys! Sit," Artemis commanded as she raced over. Wagging their tails, the dogs obeyed, but they kept their greedy pooch eyes fixed on the bag.

Aphrodite plopped down her tray, reaching the table at the same time as Artemis. "Is Adonis okay?" she gasped.

Athena kept her arms circled around the bag protectively. "Oh! He's shaking. Poor thing."

Aphrodite glared at Artemis as they both sat down. "Those brutes of yours could've hurt him! You should've left them in your room!"

"Hurt who? And they're *not* brutes!" Artemis shot back. Suddenly getting it, she pointed to the bag. "Godzooks!" she hissed at Aphrodite. "You mean you brought *him* in here? What were you thinking?"

"That I was starving?" Aphrodite replied. As Artemis calmed her dogs, Aphrodite managed to wolf down some of what was on her tray while Athena continued to hold on to the bag.

Poking her head inside, she murmured soothingly to the kitten, which seemed to calm him. When she looked up again, Pheme was zooming toward them. "Shh," she warned Aphrodite and Artemis. She nodded in Pheme's direction. "Here comes trouble."

"Whatcha got there?" the orange-haired girl asked when she reached them. She was eyeing the bag Athena clutched. Cloud letters puffed from her lips to form words that hovered above her head where everyone could read them.

"You mean the bag?" said Aphrodite. "It's mine, and . . ." Her words trailed off and she stared at Pheme blankly, as if she didn't know what else to say to make her go away.

Pheme licked her orange-glossed lips. "The dogs sure seem interested. What's in it?"

"Nothing," all three goddessgirls said quickly.

Glancing at Artemis, Pheme said, "I heard you ask Aphrodite what she was thinking bringing that bag here."

"You did? Oh, uh . . . ," Artemis said, looking blank too.

Athena thought fast. Forcing a laugh, she said, "Oh, yeah, that was funny. See, usually Artemis doesn't pay much attention to fashion. But she was just now saying that even her dogs had obviously noticed what an ugly bag this is."

"You got that right," said Pheme, considering the floppy poppy. "Ugly isn't even the word for it. It's . . . it's . . ."

"Hideous?" suggested Athena.

"Horrifying?" suggested Artemis.

"Hey—it's not that bad," Aphrodite protested. "So I made a teeny fashion error. Everybody's entitled to one. Do you have to broadcast it to the world?"

Pheme's eyes lit up at the very idea of broadcasting the news that MOA's reigning fashion queen had admitted to making a shopping mistake. "Gotta run," she said. And she hurried off to spread her gossip.

"Phew," said Athena. "That was close."

"My reputation is in ruins," Aphrodite said, only half-teasing. "But thanks for the save, Athena. It was brilliant." Then she studied her bag critically. "But *hideous*? *Horrifying*? You were both exaggerating, right?"

Athena shrugged but said nothing. She was the goddessgirl of wisdom, after all. She knew when it was best to keep quiet. Apparently the kitten did too. She'd been afraid he might squirm or yowl while Pheme was there. But Adonis had only curled up to nap. Apparently noise didn't bother him. He might not like dogs, but he didn't seem to mind being around lots of people. That was lucky!

Artemis grinned. "I can't believe Pheme actually bought that story about me having an opinion on fashion. What I know about *that* topic wouldn't fill a pitted olive." She whistled to her dogs. "Come on, boys, let's go for a walk and calm down. I'll grab a bite later."

Once Artemis and her dogs took off, Aphrodite kept an arm around the bag as she finished off her hambrosia and eggs. Athena stayed to keep her company, even though she'd already finished her own breakfast.

Later, as the two were leaving the cafeteria, they ran into one of the Norse goddesses. Athena noticed that the pretty blue eyes of the goddess in the feathered cloak were red, as if she'd been crying. Aphrodite must have noticed too, because she said, "You're Freya, right? Is something wrong?"

Freya bit her lip like she was trying to keep from crying again. "Brisingamen is missing. I took it off before I went to dinner last night. It was late when I got back to my room, and I didn't notice it was missing until this morning. I've searched and searched, but I can't find it."

"Brisingamen?" Athena echoed in surprise.

Freya touched her bare throat. "My necklace. That's its name."

"I remember! You had it on at lunch yesterday," Aphrodite exclaimed. "It's gorgeous. If I owned a necklace that wonderful, I'd give it a name too!"

"Do you need help looking for it?" Athena asked, thinking she should've asked that right away.

Freya shook her head no. "Thanks, but my friend Skadi is going to help me look again after breakfast. She thinks I just misplaced it. That's happened before, so she's probably right."

"Good luck finding it," said Aphrodite. After saying bye, she and Athena climbed the stairs to the dorm again.

"You don't think anyone *stole* Freya's necklace, do you?" Athena asked as they reached the door to her room.

"I was wondering the same thing," said Aphrodite. "I hope not, but there are a lot of strangers at MOA right now. It's possible." Just then Adonis started to mew. "Hold on, little guy," Aphrodite soothed. "We're almost home."

Athena pursed her lips. "Sorry to bring up an annoying subject, but have you talked to my dad about him yet?"

"Not yet," said Aphrodite. "I will, though. As soon as I figure out what to say that'll convince him to let Adonis stay."

That wasn't exactly the answer Athena was hoping for, but she couldn't *make* Aphrodite do the smart thing. She'd have to let her do things her way. As they parted in the dorm hall, Athena vowed to stay out of it and hope for the best.

First thing after going into her room, she checked to see if a letter had come from Heracles. But there was nothing yet. She knew he was busy. And he'd already told her he might not be back in time to see her compete. Still, she'd been crossing her fingers that he'd make it. The least he could do was send an encouraging message. After all, the elim races were today!

Well, even if he'd forgotten how to write, she hadn't. She sat at her desk and wrote him a brief note, telling him about being a tour guide, and about the new girls she'd met. She said that her practices were going fine, which they were. And that she hoped he'd make it back in time for the Olympics tomorrow. She wanted to write about Adonis, but didn't since they'd all agreed to keep him secret.

When she got to the end of her note, she hesitated. Then, before she could change her mind, she hastily scribbled *Miss you a lot*, and underlined *a lot*, three times.

Then she rolled up her letterscroll, tied it with a shiny blue ribbon, and took it to her open window. Cradling it in the palm of her outstretched hand, she chanted:

> *Come to me, breeze,*
> *And take my note, please.*
> *Then deliver it to*
> *my crush, Heracles.*

Almost instantly, a breeze whooshed up. It tickled her palm as it lifted the little scroll, then whisked it away. Just as she was about to turn from her window, Athena glanced down. Zeus's golden-winged horse, Pegasus, was standing in the courtyard. She was surprised to see a boy she didn't know calling to him. The boy's skin didn't shimmer, so he must be a mortal. Probably one of the visitors here to watch the Games.

Though tall and lanky, he looked only ten or eleven years old, she guessed. His wavy black hair hung to his shoulders. For a second he seemed kind of familiar. Had she seen him before?

No, she decided quickly. It must be that he reminded her of some of the boys at MOA. There were plenty with dark hair, including Heracles, Hades, and Apollo. Well, whoever he was, he should give up trying to befriend Pegasus. Since Zeus and Hera's wedding, that horse had become so loyal to Zeus that it shied away from everyone else.

Athena left the window and went to her closet to

change clothes. As she slipped into her navy-blue running chiton, she turned her thoughts back to the letter she'd just sent. What would Heracles think when he read her "a lot"? Was it too much? Would he think she was too stuck on him?

Maybe she shouldn't have written those words after all. She worried about it the whole time she was doing her practice run. And she forgot all about the boy she'd just seen from her window who, in the meantime, had disappeared from sight.

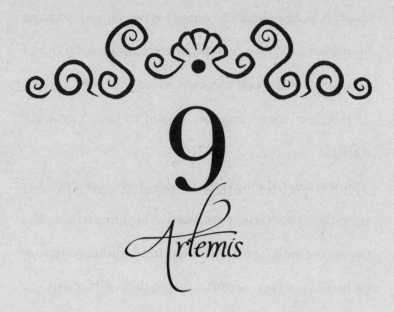

9

Artemis

Friday morning.

BY THE TIME ARTEMIS GOT BACK TO THE cafeteria after walking her dogs, Aphrodite and Athena were gone. Instead of waiting in line for a hot breakfast, she grabbed a plate from the snacks table and loaded it up with cheese, a hunk of bread, and a bunch of grapes.

The table where she and her friends usually sat was

empty now. She checked around for Apollo and Actaeon, or anyone she knew, but the cafeteria was mostly full of MOA visitors. Looked like she'd have to eat alone.

"Hey, Artemis," someone called to her. "Come eat with us!"

It was Satet, the Egyptian goddess who'd rescued her yesterday from those two snotty Amazon archers. She was sitting with Neith. Artemis almost didn't recognize them because they weren't wearing their tall crowns.

She smiled and headed for their table, glad not to have to eat alone. Satet made a big fuss over her dogs, who loved all the attention.

Pheme had told her that Satet and Neith knew some other Egyptian goddesses that Artemis and her friends had met on a trip to Cairo not long ago. She smiled, thinking of Bastet, the cat goddess she'd met there, and how they'd discussed which were better—

dogs or cats. Dogs, of course! In her opinion, anyway.

"I heard you're getting new targets for the competition tomorrow?" Neith asked.

Nodding, Artemis swallowed a bite of cheese. Then she said, "They've arrived. Just need to be unpacked."

She'd meant to do it yesterday between practices. But when she'd checked on preparations for other events, she'd discovered some problems. Such as a shortage of towels for the swimmers and improperly drawn lanes for the footraces. By the time she took care of the problems, she'd been too tired for unpacking.

"Want some help?" asked Satet.

Artemis automatically shook her head. "That's okay. I can handle it. But thanks." She didn't want them to think she wasn't up to the task of making sure the Games ran smoothly. That's why she hadn't even asked her *friends* for help.

Not that Aphrodite and Persephone could do much. They had their hands full with that kitten now. She could've asked Athena. But coordinating everything herself was the only way to know that it was all being done right. Because if something wasn't, she'd be the one Zeus would be mad at. And if he got mad enough, that would be the end of the Girl Games!

Satet's kohl-lined eyes were bright as she smiled at Artemis. "Well, if you change your mind, come find me."

"And me," added Neith.

A few hours later Artemis was walking down to the sports fields to get ready for the footrace eliminations when she spotted Athena ahead of her. "Hey, wait up!" Artemis called. Just as she caught up, the girls heard a whinny sound. They glanced back in time to see Pegasus's hooves leave the ground as he flapped his mighty golden wings.

An unfamiliar boy was running downhill after the horse, as if trying to catch him. The boy's black hair was tossed by the wind as he picked up his pace. He leaped in the air making a wild grab.

"Godsamighty!" Artemis exclaimed. "That loopy boy doesn't really expect to catch Pegasus, does he?"

"I saw him trying the same thing last night," said Athena. "Any idea who he is?"

Artemis shook her head. "But I bet I know who does." They were nearing the track now, and she nodded toward Pheme, who was standing on the sidelines. Catching her eye, Artemis waved her over.

"What's up?" Pheme asked eagerly. "Any new news?" Having exhausted her tidbit about Aphrodite's poppy-purse fashion faux pas at breakfast, she was apparently on the hunt for new gossip to spread.

"Sadly, no," said Artemis, though she wasn't really

sad about it at all. "We were actually hoping you could tell *us* something."

Pheme's face lit up. "Sure! What do you want to know?" She liked giving *out* information as much as she liked taking it *in*.

Athena pointed at the unknown boy, who was now staring dejectedly up at Pegasus as the horse flew in sweeping circles overhead. "We're wondering who that boy is."

"His name's Bellerophon," Pheme answered promptly. She gestured toward a girl doing hamstring stretches on the track. "That's his cousin over there."

"I wonder why he's so fascinated with Pegasus?" Athena mused as Pheme ran off to catch up with some-one else, who was walking back toward the Academy.

"Well, if he's hoping to ride that horse, he can forget it," Artemis said. "Pegasus is totally devoted to Zeus. And vice versa." It didn't take a genius to figure that out. Zeus was always bringing treats like apples and carrots to the winged horse. And he could often be seen in the night sky teaching Pegasus flashy tricks with the thunderbolts the horse carried for him.

"C'mon," said Athena. "The elimination races are starting."

Many of the girls competing in the Games had chosen the two-hundred-meter footrace as one of their individual events in tomorrow's Olympics, including Artemis, Athena, and Aphrodite. There would be five heats in their elims this afternoon, each with nine runners. Athena would run in the first group, and Aphrodite was in the second. Artemis wouldn't run until the fifth heat—which was the last.

Artemis cheered Athena on as the first heat began. "Go, goddessgirl!" she yelled as Athena dashed the length of the field with eight sets of feet pounding behind her. Artemis grinned at the stunned expression on her friend's face when she crossed the finish line and realized she'd won her heat.

"Way to go!" She and Athena smacked a high-five in the bottom row of the stands.

"Thanks," Athena said breathlessly. "But I don't think any of the really fast runners were in my heat."

Artemis snorted. "No way. You're faster than you think!"

Athena smiled, seeming pleased with the compliment. Then, as the next heat began, they sat to watch Aphrodite race.

She came in second, which still meant she'd get to race in the Olympics tomorrow, too. Ares was standing near the finish line during her heat. Artemis had seen a frown flicker over his face as Aphrodite crossed second. But she was glad to see him congratulate her afterward.

"Where's Adonis?" Artemis whispered to Aphrodite when she joined them in the bottom row to watch the next two heats.

Aphrodite's face clouded over. "Persephone's watching him," she said.

"Don't worry. He'll be fine. He likes her," Athena assured her.

Aphrodite's frown deepened. "That's what I'm afraid of."

Artemis and Athena looked at each other with raised eyebrows. *Uh-oh*, thought Artemis. It sounded like Aphrodite and Persephone were becoming rivals for the kitten's affection! Speaking of rivals, it had seemed like a good idea at the time when she, Aphrodite, and Athena had all signed up for the two-hundred-meter race together. But now she wondered if that might have been a mistake.

If she advanced also, they'd all wind up competing against each other in Saturday's Games. Considering the trouble brewing between Aphrodite and Persephone, it was lucky that Persephone wasn't competing in the race too!

When it was finally time for the fifth heat, Artemis took her place, crouching at the starting line. The trumpet sounded. She took off! Her legs pumped hard as she sprinted down the track. But something didn't feel right. Her rhythm was off. She could tell she was running slower than usual. Probably because she'd been working too hard and worrying too much lately. It was affecting her energy!

Through sheer determination, she crossed the finish line a fraction ahead of second place. She'd come in first! And that meant that she, Aphrodite, and Athena would all advance to race in the Olympics tomorrow.

Woo hoo! After she caught her breath, the three friends hugged in excitement. She was glad they'd all made it this far, even if it did mean they'd be competing for the same championship.

And though her shoulders sagged under the weighty thought of everything she still had to do before tomorrow's Games, she told herself that everything would be fine. She'd make sure of it!

10

Persephone

Earlier that same Friday morning,

before the elimination races.

Y OU TOOK ADONIS TO THE *CAFETERIA*!"
Persephone exclaimed when Aphrodite returned
from breakfast. Just minutes ago Persephone had
woken up alone. She'd assumed Aphrodite must've
taken the kitten outside to the bathroom. Turned out

that wasn't the only place they'd gone, though.

"Uh-huh. So?" Aphrodite replied. As soon as she let Adonis out of his woven carrier, he scampered over to his bowl and began to lap the water thirstily.

"What were you thinking?" Persephone scolded. "With all those people around, someone could've heard him. If anyone found out and told Principal Zeus, he might *banish* Adonis!"

"Nobody saw him. I was careful," Aphrodite said breezily. "Of course, Artemis's dogs did *smell* him. They came racing over, and—"

Before she could finish, Persephone practically exploded! "*Dogs?* They could've eaten Adonis in one gulp!"

"Don't go bonkers," Aphrodite said. "Athena was watching him while I was in the food line, and she—"

But Persephone tuned out the rest of her explanation.

She couldn't believe that Aphrodite had left Adonis in Athena's care. Athena was always either daydreaming about some invention, or else she had her nose stuck in a textscroll. How could she be trusted to keep a careful eye on the kitten?

"So anyway," Aphrodite finished. "No harm done. *My* kitten's fine." By now Adonis had finished drinking and was batting at the fringe on the bottom of Aphrodite's bedspread. She scooped him up and covered his little head with kisses till he squirmed to get back down.

Though her hands itched to snatch the kitten away, Persephone managed to control herself. "Don't you have elimination races soon?" she hinted.

"Not until early afternoon," Aphrodite replied.

"I can watch Adonis while you're gone," Persephone offered quickly.

Aphrodite seemed to hesitate for a moment. "All right," she said finally. She sounded reluctant.

Persephone looked longingly at Adonis. "I'll go grab some breakfast now, but I'll be right back," she said. After tearing her eyes away from the kitten, she turned to leave.

"Shouldn't you change out of your pj's first?" Aphrodite called to her.

Persephone popped back inside, grinning in embarrassment. "Thanks for the save. I'm used to being at home. I always have breakfast in my pj's there."

That friendly moment smoothed things over between them a bit, which made Persephone feel better. She'd been jittery ever since they'd begun arguing over the kitten. It was no fun fighting with one of her best friends!

When Persephone returned from breakfast, she

and Aphrodite chatted, read magazines, and played with Adonis together until it was time for Aphrodite to leave for the track. "See you after the elims," Aphrodite said, heading out the door.

"Good luck," Persephone told her. "No need to hurry back." As soon as Aphrodite left, she fed Adonis his lunch. She wasn't really hungry herself, since she'd eaten a big breakfast. But while he crunched on his cat chow, she snacked on a bag of ambrosia-flavored chips she and Aphrodite had bought at the Market last night.

Then she retrieved the red ribbon she'd borrowed from Aphrodite's drawer before. "You like it when it's just the two of us, don't you, sweetie?" she cooed as they both enjoyed a game of "chase the ribbon snake." Adonis was just *so* cute!

Aphrodite had been gone for nearly an hour when Persephone suddenly remembered that she was supposed to practice with Hades at one o'clock! She'd been having so much fun with the kitten she'd forgotten.

Leaping up, she went to the window to check the sundial in the courtyard below. It was already a few minutes past one, but she didn't see Hades waiting for her. *Good.* He must be a little late too. She started out of the room to go tell him they'd have to postpone her practice. Then she turned back to look at Adonis.

It probably wasn't a good idea to leave him alone, even for a few minutes. He might get lonely and start meowing. Someone would hear.

Making a quick decision, she grabbed the woven bag Aphrodite had left on her bed. Gently, she placed Adonis on top of the heart pillow inside. "We're going for a ride, cutie," she singsonged.

As she picked up the bag, she noticed the floppy yellow poppy design on the front, which she hadn't seen till now. *Ye gods,* she thought. Yellow was one of her favorite colors, but this bag was mega-tacky. Aphrodite usually had way better taste.

Persephone hurried downstairs with the kitten. But when she got outside to the courtyard, Hades still wasn't there. Nobody else was either. Almost everyone was over at the sports fields today for the elim races.

Suddenly she heard a loud *crack* at the edge of the courtyard. She jumped around in time to see the ground split open. Four black stallions pushed up through the gap, pulling a chariot.

"Hades!" She would know his horses anywhere. Besides, who else would be riding up from the Underworld?

"Whoa!" he shouted to his stallions. As his chariot came to a stop, Hades reached up with one hand and swept back a dark lock of hair that had fallen across his eyes. It was a familiar motion that always caused Persephone's heart to flutter a little.

"Sorry I'm late for your practice," he called down to her as he steadied the horses. "Big emergency down in the Underworld. Three Titans escaped Tartarus. I've got them rounded up, but I need to hurry back so I can finish giving them a talking-to."

"Okay," Persephone said, relieved to be off the hook. "We can cancel practice."

The stallion closest to her sniffed at the bag holding Adonis, then shook its massive head and snorted. Persephone drew back.

Adonis didn't make a sound inside the bag. Maybe he was tired from all their playing and had fallen asleep. She hoped he wasn't scared, though. She edged away, turning to go back inside. "Guess I'll see you—"

"Wait! Actually, I could use your help. Those Titans

are really in a tizzy down there, and your mere presence always has a calming effect on them. Could you come? I asked some of the shades to mark out a long-jump pit for you."

"Shades," Persephone knew, was another name for the souls of the dead.

"You can practice while I finish up," Hades added. He reached a hand down to her, waiting to help her into the chariot.

"But . . . I can't," Persephone protested, stepping back.

"Why not?" Hades considered her with a frown, and then stiffened. "Is it your mom? Did she decide we can't hang out anymore?"

Persephone shook her head, her voice softening. "No, nothing like that," she assured him. She understood his concern, though. When her mom had first found out that she was friends with him—a godboy that many regarded (wrongly) as the Bad Boy of the Underworld—she'd practically gone ballistic. That had hurt his feelings.

But eventually they'd all come to an understanding. These days her mom gave her a little more space to make her own decisions about who she hung out with and where she went. Persephone had visited the Underworld many times by now, and her mom was fine with it.

"Well, then . . ." Hades was eyeing her curiously, undoubtedly waiting for her to explain why she couldn't come.

Persephone's hands tightened on the handles of the poppy bag. What excuse could she use? Hades could usually tell when she was fibbing. "I . . . um . . . need to give this bag to Aphrodite, but she's not back from the track yet." There, that was true.

Just then Hades' stallions, probably anxious to be off again, stamped the ground with their hooves and snorted. They must've startled Adonis awake because he began to wiggle. "Mee—OWW!"

Hades stared at the bag, his eyes widening. "Do you have a cat in there?"

"Um." Caught, Persephone spilled the truth. What else could she do? Luckily, she knew she could trust Hades to keep Adonis a secret. As she explained about the kitten, she opened the bag to let Hades see him.

"Cute little guy," Hades said. He snapped his fingers. "I know. Let's just take him with us."

Persephone hesitated, weighing her options. She glanced one last time in the direction of the sports fields, hoping to see Aphrodite returning. Seeing no sign of her, Athena, or Artemis, she figured the elimination footraces must still be going on. She reached inside the bag to stroke the fur on Adonis's back. "Think he'll be safe?" she asked.

Hades nodded. "Sure—if you keep an eye on him."

"Oh, I will," she said earnestly.

"All right, then," he said, grinning. "Hop aboard."

Persephone took his hand and stepped into the chariot. Just as his stallions leaped downward through the crack in the ground, she happened to glance back up at the girls' dorm on the fourth floor. Someone was standing at one of the windows in the stairwell looking down at them. There was a reflection on the glass, so she couldn't tell who.

Whoever it was couldn't have seen Adonis, though. He was still safely tucked away in Aphrodite's bag. As the chariot headed down to the Underworld again,

Persephone held the bag close, cuddling the kitten. She could feel his soft warmth and the gentle rumble of his purr. How sweet!

Underworld could be a forbidding place, but Adonis should be perfectly safe under her care. Hades had even said so. Certainly the kitten would be safer than he'd been in the cafeteria this morning with all those people and Artemis's dogs around! With any luck, Hades would solve his Titan problem quickly and they'd be back here before Aphrodite even knew they were gone.

11

Aphrodite

Friday, early afternoon.

YOU JUST NEED TO FOCUS MORE," SAID ARES.

Aphrodite nodded. "Mm-hm." It was after the elimination races, and she, Athena, and Artemis were walking back to the Academy with Ares, Apollo, and Actaeon.

Unfortunately, Ares was spending the whole time

making suggestions about how she could better her time in tomorrow's race. She pretended to listen. But thinking about her running technique actually just made her want to, well, *run away*!

She smiled to see Artemis and Actaeon chatting so easily. Those two were still shy about even holding hands. But she knew a blossoming crush when she saw one. And though she wasn't directly responsible for getting them together, she was always delighted to see people in like—especially her best friends!

Apollo and Athena were talking about the eliminations. Boring, but maybe it would take Athena's mind off Heracles' absence. Really, it was too bad the boys' wrestling team couldn't have rescheduled their meet for a time that didn't conflict with the girls' very first Olympics!

It was several seconds before Aphrodite realized

that Ares had stopped his coach-speak to study her face. Finally he said, "You aren't listening to me, are you?"

"Huh?" Aphrodite felt her cheeks redden. "Sorry. I was distracted."

He reached for her hand, giving it an encouraging squeeze. "You're going to look good out there tomorrow. Don't worry."

Aphrodite threaded her fingers through his. "I know," she said, thinking fondly of the sparkly pink running chiton she'd bought. She hadn't worn it for the heats today. She was saving it for tomorrow's Olympic race!

"You're a good runner," Ares persisted. "And with a little more effort, you could be a *great* runner."

Aphrodite nodded. It wasn't the first time he'd told her that. But as he began to talk about racing, her mind drifted off again—this time to thoughts of Adonis. A fond, wistful smile curved her lips. She was so preoccupied that she didn't notice the strange looks Ares was giving her.

"What are you thinking about?" he asked suddenly. He sounded kind of jealous!

"Oh, nothing. No one." She pulled her hand away, sending him a guilty look. She felt bad for lying, but she'd promised not to tell anyone about Adonis.

"Hmph!" he said, looking weirdly suspicious for some reason. She didn't get a chance to ask him what was bothering him. Because as soon as they were inside the Academy, the boys split off and ambled toward the cafeteria for a late lunch.

The girls went upstairs to change clothes first. "See you in a few," Athena called as she opened her dorm room door.

"Later," Aphrodite and Artemis called back as they continued down the hall. As they got closer to their rooms, Artemis's dogs began to scratch at the inside of her door and bark excitedly. "They know your footsteps, don't they?" Aphrodite said.

Artemis grinned. "Yep."

Aphrodite wondered if Adonis would recognize her footsteps, too. Imagining the kitten eagerly waiting for her and looking overjoyed to see her, she threw open the door to her room.

"I'm back!" she announced dramatically. Silence greeted her. Persephone and Adonis weren't there! Immediately she panicked. Glancing around, she saw that the poppy bag she'd flung onto her bed was also missing. After giving her such a hard time about taking Adonis to the cafeteria that morning, had Persephone dared take him with her to lunch?

Yanking a favorite teal chiton from her closet, Aphrodite changed quickly. Then she zipped downstairs to the cafeteria. Standing just inside the door, she scanned the crowd. No Persephone.

She was about to go search elsewhere when she spotted Pheme. She could hardly believe she was doing this, but she actually went over to speak to the girl. "Have you seen Persephone?" she asked her.

Pheme's eyes lit up like they always did when she had knowledge that someone else wanted. "She went off with Hades in his chariot."

Aphrodite jerked her head back in surprise. *This* was unexpected news! "What? When? Where did they go?" she asked anxiously.

"They left about a half hour ago," Pheme said. "I only saw them from a dorm window, but I'm pretty sure they were headed for the Underworld."

Aphrodite lost her cool. "WHAT?" Telling herself to calm down, she took a couple of deep breaths. After all, only half of what Pheme said usually turned out to be true. "What makes you think that's where they were going?" she asked.

Pheme shrugged. "Well, it looked that way. I mean, their chariot did disappear through a crack in the ground. Oh, and she was carrying that ugly, um, I mean, that *big* bag of yours with the yellow flower."

Aphrodite gritted her teeth. She knew what that meant. Persephone had Adonis. And it was even worse than she thought. She hadn't simply taken him to the cafeteria; she'd taken him to the Underworld. Talk about an unsafe place for a kitten!

Underworld was full of icky, scary stuff like stinky marshes and rivers of molten lava. Not to mention Hades' ferocious three-headed dog, Cerberus.

Remembering his sharp, pointy teeth, she shuddered, fearing for Adonis.

Pheme's eyes gleamed. "What's wrong? Is there a problem between you and Persephone? Maybe you'd like to tell me about it. Your secrets will be safe with me. Honest." Lifting a hand, she twisted her thumb and finger together at the corner of her orange-glossed lips, as if turning a key to lock them shut.

Aphrodite rolled her eyes. Entrusting a secret to Pheme was pretty much the same as standing on the stage of a crowded amphitheater and shouting it out. "Everything's fine between us, thanks," she fibbed.

"If you say so," Pheme said, sounding disappointed. Just then, Freya happened to walk by, still looking weepy. Changing the subject, Pheme leaned closer and murmured, "Poor thing. Did you hear that her necklace is missing? Possibly even stolen."

"Yeah, well, I wouldn't be surprised. There's a lot of that going around," Aphrodite said, thinking of the kitten-napping that Persephone had pulled off.

Pheme shot her a weird look, like she wasn't quite sure what to make of her response. Before the girl had a chance to pry further, Aphrodite said, "Well, I'm starving . . . see you later."

With a little wave, she took off for the snack table, not noticing the calculating expression on Pheme's face as she watched her go. The kind of expression that meant she was trying to add two and two together. And since Pheme liked to exaggerate everything, the answer she'd come up with was likely to be *wrong*!

Aphrodite grabbed an apple from the table, her mind racing wildly. Even before now she'd begun to suspect that Persephone wanted Adonis for her own. Hadn't she stolen him from Aphrodite's bed last night?

What if Persephone planned to say she lost Adonis in the Underworld, but then really took him to live at her house? Would she be that devious? Maybe. She adored that kitten!

The more Aphrodite thought about it, the more she convinced herself that she was right about Persephone's intentions. Determined to confront her so-called friend, she decided not to wait for her return. She would go to the Underworld herself and take Adonis back. But to do that, she would need transportation.

While munching her apple, she raced up to the fourth floor and then to her room. She tossed away the apple core and grabbed a ceramic figurine from her shelf. It was small enough to fit in her hand and was made up of two swans side by side, pulling a golden cart behind them. With their faces turned toward each other and their orange beaks pressed together, their gracefully curved necks formed a perfect heart.

She dashed for the door but turned back at the last minute. Grabbing a handful of dry cat chow, she stuffed it into a small sack for when she found Adonis. Which she would!

Holding the figurine, Aphrodite hurried downstairs again. Once in the courtyard, she stroked a fingertip over each swan's snowy white back. Then she gently placed the figurine on one of the courtyard's marble tiles and stepped back, chanting:

> *"Feathered swans, wild at heart.*
> *Spread your wings to fly my cart!"*

As if awakening from a deep, magical sleep, the two swans fluttered and shook their heads. Their wings unfurled and the swans grew and grew until they were ten feet tall with wingspans of twenty feet. The golden cart, which sparkled with encrusted jewels, had also enlarged.

Hopping into the cart, Aphrodite called out: *"To the Underworld!"* The swans gave a startled honk at this destination but quickly obeyed.

12

Athena

Friday, early afternoon.

Y AYYY!" ATHENA WAS OVERJOYED TO FIND A letterscroll on the floor beneath her window when she got back to her room after winning her heat in the two-hundred-meter elims. She dashed over and grabbed it up. Eagerly she unrolled it. Sure enough, it was from Heracles:

DEAR ATHENA,

TODAY I WILL BATTLE ANTAEUS, THE
TOUGHEST WRESTLER ON THE GIANTS'
TEAM. EVERYONE SAYS HE'S INVINCIBLE,
BUT I'M SURE I CAN BEAT HIM.

Athena smiled to herself. No one would ever accuse
Heracles of lacking confidence. And no doubt he
would win his match. After all, he'd won the wrestling
championship against a giant in the boys' Olympics not
long ago!

I HOPE TO BE BACK TOMORROW IN TIME TO
SEE YOU COMPETE. SOME OF US GUYS ARE
PLANNING AN AFTER-THE-GAMES SURPRISE I
THINK YOU'LL LIKE.

SEE YOU SOON!

HERACLES

XOXO

Athena traced the *X*s and *O*s with a fingertip, smiling softly. She guessed that meant he missed her "a lot"

140

too. She reread the part about an after-the-Games surprise, wondering what it could be. She was still wondering as she went downstairs for lunch a half hour later.

Just before she went into the cafeteria, she heard someone rushing down the staircase behind her. Turning, she saw Aphrodite race toward the Academy's bronze front doors. She was holding her swan cart figurine. Before Athena could call to her, Aphrodite pushed through the doors to the outside. Where was she off to in such a hurry?

Athena was already in the lunch line when she spotted Artemis holding a full tray and heading toward the goddessgirls' usual table. Wagging their tails, her dogs dodged between students to follow her.

"Here you go." The eight-armed lunch lady was ladling up bowls of celestial soup with four of her hands and handing them out with her other four hands. Thanking her, Athena took the bowl she was offered and grabbed a few crackers, too. As she went to sit with Artemis, she scanned the room.

"Have you seen Persephone?" she asked as she sat down.

Artemis blew on a spoonful of soup. "Nuh-uh. She probably ate earlier."

"Yeah, probably," Athena agreed. "Do you think Aphrodite's eaten already too? I saw her going outside just now."

Artemis shrugged. "Must have." Changing the subject, she asked, "So do you think Heracles and the rest of the wrestling team will make it back in time for the Games tomorrow?"

"Fingers crossed." Athena took his letterscroll from her pocket and handed it to Artemis. She'd brought it, wanting to get her friends' takes on what the surprise Hercules had mentioned could be.

When she reached the bottom of the letter, Artemis grinned and raised an eyebrow. "X-O-X-O?"

Athena felt her cheeks go warm. "What do you think the guys are planning?" she asked to cover her embarrassment. "A party for the girls?"

"Could be," Artemis said distractedly. Nodding toward the cafeteria door beyond Athena, she added, "Hey, look. There's that boy again—the one we saw chasing Pegasus on our way to the track this morning. What was his name again? Bellboy? Bellbottom?"

"Bellerophon," Athena said, without turning around.

"Well, don't look now," said Artemis. "But he's coming this way."

Of course, Athena immediately looked over. Catching her eye, Bellerophon smiled and waved. "You're

Athena, right?" he asked her when he reached their table. "Zeus's daughter?"

Athena nodded.

"Can we talk?" he asked. Flicking Artemis a quick glance, he added, "Alone?"

Artemis shrugged and clanked her spoon into her empty bowl. "I need to get going anyway. I've got practice. Plus, there's a shipment I need to unpack before tomorrow and some other stuff to check on too."

Picking up her tray, she stood. Her dogs, who'd been lying under the table, scrambled to their feet to follow her. As Athena watched her friend go, she wondered if she should've offered to help out. But Artemis didn't seem to want any help.

Hearing a chair scrape the floor, she looked over to see Bellerophon sitting at her table. "Sorry to bug you," he began, "but I need a favor."

Athena stiffened. "A favor?" she asked cautiously. Because she was Zeus's daughter, some people figured she had an "in" with him. Usually the *favors* they wanted involved her asking him to do something for them.

Bellerophon hesitated. Maybe he sensed her sudden coolness toward him. "It's about Pegasus."

"Um-hm?" said Athena, taking another spoonful of soup. Having seen him with the winged horse, she had a feeling she knew what was coming.

He looked around the cafeteria as if to make sure no one was listening. Then he leaned forward and whispered, "I want to ride him."

"Wish I could help," she told him. "But you'll have to ask my dad. Pegasus belongs to him."

Bellerophon frowned. "But—*you* are supposed to help me."

"Says who?" she asked, cocking her head.

"Says my dream!" he blurted out. "You were in it. You gave me the golden bridle!"

Dream? Golden bridle? Athena stared at him with shocked recognition. So it wasn't Heracles she'd seen in that strange dream she'd had when she'd fallen asleep at her desk yesterday. It was this boy!

A dream wasn't anything to be taken lightly—especially since they'd apparently shared the same one. If she'd appeared in this boy's dream and made a promise to help him—it meant something!

Athena tapped her spoon lightly on her bowl, thinking. "Tell you what. How about if I introduce you to my dad? Then *you* can ask him if it's okay to ride Pegasus."

Bellerophon looked a little nervous at the idea, which was no surprise. Almost everyone, even Athena herself, found Zeus intimidating. His height, his muscles, his electric touch, and his status as King of the Gods made sure of that.

"Okay," Bellerophon agreed finally.

Athena rose from the table and picked up her tray. "C'mon," she said. After placing her tray in the tray return, she led the boy to the front office.

Nine-headed Ms. Hydra, Zeus's administrative assistant, was eating her lunch at the counter there when they entered. Her orange head swiveled toward them, but her purple head continued to gulp down the yambrosia she was spooning up. The rest of her heads were keeping tabs on her office work.

"If you're here to see Principal Zeus, you'll have to come back later," her orange head told them. "He's in a meeting."

Athena peered over at Ms. Hydra's pink head, a question in her eyes. "With the king of Lycia," the pink head mouthed silently. Pinky, as students called this head, was almost as gossipy as Pheme, at least when it came to Zeus news.

Suddenly there was a terrible crash from Zeus's inner office. His loud voice boomed through the closed door. "Thunderation! You say it may be coming this way?"

All eighteen of Ms. Hydra's eyes went wide at once. "Oh! This sounds bad. Could mean disaster for MOA!" her gray head wailed. This one was her worrywart head.

Trouble? What was she talking about? Athena wondered. And *what* was headed this way? But before she could ask, another huge *BOOM* came from Zeus's office. Her dad must be throwing things again. He only did that when he was upset. *Very* upset.

"Maybe now's not a good time," Bellerophon whispered.

Athena nodded. "Probably not. Let's go."

As the two of them went into the main hall, a couple of students pushed in through the bronze doors up ahead. Athena heard a loud whinny from outside. Instantly Bellerophon's face lit up. "Pegasus!" He raced outside.

Athena quickly followed, watching as Bellerophon zoomed down the granite steps that led to the courtyard. Taking Pegasus by surprise, he leaped onto the horse's back and wrapped his arms around its neck.

Athena gasped, half-expecting Pegasus to shake the boy off. Instead, the winged horse only stood calmly, as if waiting for something more to happen. Slowly and purposefully, it turned its head and gazed directly at her!

This was exactly what had happened in her dream, she realized. An urge came over her to complete the dream for real now. Because surely this must mean that she was *destined* to grant Bellerophon's wish. Forgetting all about asking Zeus, Athena swept her arm through the air in an arc, chanting:

> *Behold! Behold!*
>
> *A bridle of gold.*
>
> *Let it gentle the ride.*
>
> *Of the horseman—uh, horseboy—astride.*

As the last word of her chant died away, a shiny golden bridle magically appeared. It settled over the top of Pegasus's head. Bellerophon glanced over, sending Athena a grateful smile. Then he took off, galloping into the air. "Yahoooo!" His shout of joy startled several students crossing the courtyard.

"When will you be back!" Athena remembered to call out. But he didn't seem to hear. As horse and rider sailed away, the king of Lycia himself came stomping down the granite stairs past her. Without a word, he leaped into his chariot and drove off.

Uh-oh! Now that his visitor had gone, what if Zeus left his office and came looking for Pegasus? When he was in a stormy mood, there was nothing he liked better than to go sky-riding and toss around his thunderbolts.

Athena ran to the olive grove at the far side of the courtyard just in case Zeus did come out. There, she nervously awaited Bellerophon's return—hoping she wasn't going to find herself in big trouble for impulsively granting his wish.

13

Artemis

Friday, mid-afternoon.

ARTEMIS WAS AT THE ARCHERY RANGE, training her three silver arrows to fly straight and true, when she heard a whinny. It was followed by the loud *whoosh* of wings directly overhead. As she released an arrow, she took her eye off the target for half a second to look up.

There in the sky she was astonished to see Pegasus with a rider on his back who clearly wasn't Zeus. It looked like that kid, Bellybutton—or whatever his name was—from lunch. How had he gotten Pegasus to give him a ride? she wondered as horse and boy disappeared into the distance.

"Artemis!" Apollo's sharp call interrupted her thoughts. She glanced over her shoulder at him and Actaeon. "You're not focusing!" her brother said sternly. Gazing toward the target, she saw what he meant. She'd not only missed the bull's-eye, she'd missed the entire target! Actaeon went to retrieve her arrow.

"Sorry," she said. Apollo was right. She couldn't afford to be sloppy. Now she'd have to train that arrow to fly right all over again.

It was just so hard to concentrate on practicing right now. She had so much else to do, and it wasn't getting done. For one thing, the targets here on the range were too holey from arrow tip punctures. She needed to unpack the boxes of new targets to replace them. But she also needed to get to bed early tonight. Because the Girl Games were tomorrow!

Actaeon ran up to her with the arrow she'd shot. His hand brushed hers as he gave it to her.

"Thanks." She felt herself smile in a goo-goo way at him. She couldn't help it! But she hoped Apollo hadn't noticed. She didn't want him to start teasing her right in front of her crush.

"No problem," said Actaeon. Then he looked over at Apollo. "That's enough practice. I think we could all use a break."

"Yeah," Artemis agreed. "There are some things I need to do."

Apollo rolled his eyes. "Oh, all right." He whistled to

her dogs, who'd been napping in the shade under the stands. "I'll take them for a run, then drop them by your room," he offered.

"That would be so great," said Artemis, relieved. As grouchy as Apollo had been lately, she knew it was only because he wanted her to do well in the Games. She just wasn't sure if it was for her sake or his. Maybe both. She was too tired to figure it out.

Feeling Actaeon's gaze on her, she looked up into his concerned gray eyes. "You look stressed out. Is there anything I can do? Anything you need?" he asked.

Maybe a hug? Artemis thought. Honestly, she felt overwhelmed and really *could* use a hug right now. But she'd rather die from a scorpion sting than ask!

Actaeon was staring at her kind of weirdly now, like they were the only two people on the entire range. Had he guessed her thoughts? "Maybe—" he started to say.

155

Apollo butted in. "Hey, Actaeon, don't forget. We have that . . . *thing* . . . to do."

"Thing?" Actaeon glanced at Apollo, then seemed to remember. "Oh, yeah. *That* thing."

His eyes held secrets when he looked at Artemis again. "But I can skip it," he told her. "I mean, if you need help."

He was so sweet to offer. She wanted to tell him the truth. That she really could use help unpacking the shipment Hermes had delivered yesterday afternoon. But she didn't want him to know she wasn't as on top of things as she should be. Besides, it wasn't fair to mess up Actaeon's plans just because she'd let her own stuff get out of control.

"No, that's okay." She stepped back. If she wasn't careful, she might accidentally give herself away. If he was just being friendly, how embarrassing would it be if she'd actually asked for a hug? *Ye gods!* Apollo would have teased her to death over that. She was glad neither boy could read her mind.

Splitting off from them, Artemis started toward the gym. On the way, she paused to watch Skadi aim and release an arrow. *Zzzing!* Bull's-eye. It confirmed her belief that Skadi and the Amazons would be her biggest competition in tomorrow's contest.

Artemis cupped her hands around her mouth and called, "Awesome shot!"

The Norse goddessgirl's long blond hair fluttered as she turned her way. "Thanks!" she called back. As the girl drew another arrow from her quiver, Artemis moved off.

The Egyptian and Amazon girls were hanging around the edge of the range, watching the other archers. Satet and Neith were sitting cross-legged on the grass and said hi to Artemis as she passed. "Where you off to?" asked Satet. She was wearing her red crown again.

"To the gym," Artemis told her. "Got some supplies to unpack."

"Need help?" Satet asked.

"Yeah, we're done practicing for now," added Neith. She picked up her antelope-horn crown from her lap and put it on as she stood.

Satet rose too and dusted the grass off her skirt. Glancing at Penthe and Hippolyta, who were standing nearby, she said, "You'll help too, right?"

The two Amazon girls gave her a startled look. It was probably the last thing they wanted to do. But before they could come up with any excuses, Satet turned back to Artemis. "See? Plenty of help here."

Artemis hesitated. These girls were guests. They

shouldn't *have* to help. But she had to admit, she could sure use some. Even the Amazons' reluctant help would be better than nothing!

Besides, Satet *had* offered to help once before. For all she knew, it might be rude to turn down such an offer in Egyptian culture. Just in case, Artemis said, "I'd love some help. Thanks."

"No problem. Lead on," said Satet. She and Neith headed off with Artemis to the gym. Sighing, the two Amazon girls followed.

Just as they got there, Principal Zeus and Professor Ladon, who taught Beast-ology at MOA, came around the corner from the front of the gym. They were so deep in conversation, they didn't seem to notice the girls standing by the side doors. Zeus looked to be in a thunderous mood.

Artemis's eyes followed him and the professor. As

the other girls chattered among themselves, she saw Zeus shake a fist in the air. "—could absolutely ruin the Games!" she heard him declare.

Her heart began to beat fast. What was he talking about? *What* could ruin the Games?"

She listened hard to hear Professor Ladon's response, but only caught a few words of it as he and Zeus moved on. Still, those words made her shudder down to her toes: "—have to cancel them."

Cancel the Games? No-o! She glanced around at the other girls, trying to gauge if any of them had heard. But they were still chatting away. While she was practically having a heart attack, they were blissfully unaware.

Her hands shook as she fumbled in her pocket for the key Zeus had given her to unlock the door. Was this her fault? Had Zeus discovered some humongous problem she wasn't aware of? Something she should've taken care of? Only, what could be big enough to cancel the Games? Her shaking fingers pulled out the key, but she was so freaked out that she dropped it.

"Butterfingers," muttered Penthe as it clinked against the stone step they were standing on.

Artemis ignored her snootiness. She had way bigger things to worry about! Scooping up the key, she managed to unlock the doors.

Inside the gym's storage room, the boxes of supplies were sitting just where she and Hermes had stacked them. Artemis was surprised anew that there were so many boxes. She didn't remember ordering this much stuff.

"Where should we start?" Satet asked.

"Open the ones labeled 'beanbag animals,'" Artemis said, pointing at a group of boxes. "They're for the relay races."

161

"There sure are a lot with that label," said Neith as she sorted through the boxes.

She was right, Artemis noticed. That was strange. They'd only ordered twenty stuffed beanbag animals to hand off in the relays. Those should've all fit in a couple of boxes.

"Oh, how fun!" exclaimed Satet as she tore open the box Artemis handed her and saw what was inside. She lifted out a small stuffed unicorn with a rainbow-colored horn and showed it to the other girls.

"It's adorable!" Neith agreed. Diving into the box she'd just opened, she came up with a little green crocodile. "Isn't this one cute!" She hugged the crocodile to her chest.

Penthe plunged both hands into her box. Then she held up a silver-gray horse in one hand and an orange cat in the other. Artemis could tell she liked them, but of course Penthe wouldn't admit it. "Are these going to be prizes?" Penthe asked instead.

"Not exactly," said Artemis. "The runners on the relay teams will be handing them off instead of batons." She ducked her head, expecting laughter.

But, instead, the girls were delighted. She didn't have the heart to tell them there was a chance the Games could be called off. And anyway, it might not happen, right? So why start any rumors? Maybe she had misunderstood Zeus and the professor. Until she heard otherwise from them, she was going to carry on getting ready for the Games and hope for the best!

"Can the teams choose which animal they want to use in the race?" Hippolyta asked. She was cuddling a floppy-eared brown-and-white toy dog in her arms.

"Sure," said Artemis, a bit startled. "Good idea." It amazed her that these tough Amazon warrior girls were going crazy over stuffed animals. Satet and Neith were too. To think that she'd been worried that true athletes might consider them too girly! Aphrodite's idea had been a good one after all.

Digging into another box, Artemis finally found a packing slip. It read:

TWENTY BOXES OF ASSORTED STUFFED

BEANBAG ANIMALS.

FOR DELIVERY TO MOUNT OLYMPUS ACADEMY.

Her eyes bugged. Oh no! There were supposed to be twenty *animals*. Not twenty *boxes* of animals. She knew she should've done all the ordering herself! She'd let Aphrodite take care of the relay race order, and she'd made a mistake. Artemis supposed they could return the extra boxes. But then she got an even better idea!

"At the end of the Games, every girl will get to keep one of the animals," she announced. "In fact, you can each choose your favorite now, instead of waiting till tomorrow, since you helped unpack."

At this, there were more squeals of delight. Artemis could hardly believe it when Penthe kissed the silver-gray horse, then pretended to make it trot across her lap.

While the girls finished sorting the animals—there were ten in each box, making two hundred altogether—they talked about their cultures. Artemis was fascinated to learn that the Amazons had a queen, not a king.

"Why would we need a king?" Penthe said scornfully. "Boys are considered dorks in our culture. We're way better at sports and smarter than they are. It's better that we make the rules."

Artemis liked that Amazonian culture valued girls. But if she thought some boys were annoying, she didn't think they were dorks. Well, not all of them, anyway.

And if Penthe really felt that way, then why had she made goo-goo eyes at Actaeon yesterday morning? Her stomach churned just remembering. Luckily, her gloomy thoughts were interrupted when Athena burst into the room.

"Thank godness I found you!" she exclaimed, looking at Artemis. She was breathing hard, like she'd been running. And she seemed upset.

"What's wrong?" Artemis asked, jumping up. Had Zeus told Athena he was canceling the Games?

"I'll explain later, but can you come with me? Now?" Athena asked, not even glancing toward the other four girls. She obviously didn't want to say what was bothering her in front of them.

"Want us to stay and unpack the rest of these boxes?" Satet asked.

"That's okay," Artemis told her. "I'll finish later."
If there *was* a later where the Games were concerned!
Anyway, Zeus was trusting her with the gym key and she
needed to lock up behind them.

After everyone was finally out of the gym and
Artemis and Athena were alone, words poured from
Athena. "You know that boy, Bellerophon?"

"Yeah, I saw him flying on Pegasus earlier," Artemis
said, shutting the loading dock doors and fishing out her
key. What did Bellerophon have to do with the Games
getting canceled? she wondered.

"Really? Which way?" asked Athena, scanning the
sky.

"East."

Athena glanced hopefully in that direction, but
then her shoulders slumped. "He's disappeared. With
Pegasus! They've been gone an hour now, and my dad

is going to throw a thunderbolt fit of epic proportions when he finds out!"

"Well, that's Bellerophon's problem, isn't it?" Artemis said. "I mean, he shouldn't have—"

"No! You don't understand. I have to find him! Can you help me?" Athena looked like she was about to cry. "I tried to get help from Aphrodite and Persephone. But they weren't in the dorm or out on the field. Skadi told me she'd seen you head here. I'm so sorry to bother you. I know you have a lot going on," she added all in a rush.

"Are you kidding? I'm glad to help." Secretly, Artemis was big-time relieved that *this* was the problem Athena wanted help with. She hadn't come to say that Zeus had canceled the Games after all! Still, she didn't see why Athena was so worried about Bellerophon and Pegasus. Bellerophon seemed like a natural rider, so what trouble could he really get into? But if Athena needed help, she would help her!

"C'mon," she said, setting off across the sports fields for the Academy. "You'll need some support when you tell your dad they're late."

"No!" Athena grabbed her arm, paling.

Artemis froze as she suddenly guessed something. "You mean Principal Zeus didn't give his permission?"

"Right. And I sort of helped Bellerophon take Pegasus," Athena admitted.

Now it was Artemis's turn to go pale. Had Zeus already heard about this? Is that why he'd mentioned maybe canceling the Games? She felt a flash of anger toward Athena. This was all her fault! But maybe there was still a way to set things right.

Without another word, she stuck two fingers in her mouth and whistled. At her summons, her four milk-white deer with golden horns came leaping to her side, pulling a chariot behind them. "Let's go find them," she told Athena.

Piling into the chariot, they took off. As they flew over Mount Olympus, Athena explained about her and Bellerophon's dream. And about how she'd helped make it come true. As Artemis listened, her anger toward her friend softened. Shared dreams were something to be taken seriously. But Zeus, of course, didn't know about the dream.

Sailing upward, they searched the skies for the missing horse and rider. But all they saw was endless, empty blue stretching in every direction.

Athena groaned. "If we don't find Pegasus before my dad does, I'm dead."

No, the Games were dead, thought Artemis. To

punish them, Zeus would probably cancel tomorrow's Games for sure—dream or no dream! She gritted her teeth. That just couldn't happen. They'd find Pegasus and set things right. They *had* to. The Girl Games must go on!

14

Persephone

Friday afternoon.

WHOA!" HADES CALLED TO HIS FOUR BLACK

stallions as they arrived in the Underworld. After a half

hour of travel from MOA, his chariot had come to a

halt in a field of asphodel. The star-shaped white flow-

ers, which stood atop tall stalks, grew abundantly down

here. They were the favorite food of the Dead.

Persephone inhaled the flowers' sweet fragrance as Hades lifted her down from his chariot. She clutched the woven bag with Adonis inside, keeping him safe until she stood on the ground. Not far away, she could hear the Titans griping and yelling.

"Thanks for coming, Perseph," Hades told her. "I know your presence will calm those Titans and make them easier for me to handle. After I deal with them and the damage they caused on their rampage, I'll be back. Oh, and the long-jump practice pit is over there." Just before he dashed off, he pointed to a place a short distance away where the field had been mowed.

Persephone smiled, watching him go. Some boys were cute, she thought, but Hades was darkly *handsome*. If he acted more serious than other boys, it was only because he had so much responsibility down here in the Underworld. But she liked that about him.

Adonis started to wriggle, so she lifted him from the bag, holding him carefully with his feet tucked up under him. In the next asphodel field over, she spotted some shades. Their wispy humanlike figures moved slowly, harvesting the blossoms. If they didn't seem exactly happy, they didn't seem *un*happy, either. She supposed that made sense. During their mortal lives, they'd done equal amounts of good *and* evil.

When Adonis squirmed to get down, Persephone lowered him to the ground. After sniffing at the flowers, he scampered off through the field. She kept pace with him, laughing.

Eventually the kitten tired, and she gave him some water dipped from a clear stream. Then she set him on the pillow inside the woven bag. He immediately curled up for a nap. Leaving the top of the bag open, she carried it over to the long-jump pit the shades had built. She set the bag to one side, where she could keep an eye on it while she practiced.

As she did her jumps, she started to worry a little. Not about Hades. She didn't doubt that he could handle the Titans—he was godboy of the Underworld, after all. And he had lots of help, including his three-headed dog, Cerberus, who made sure that no one who belonged in the Underworld ever escaped.

No, it was Aphrodite she was worried about. What would she think if she arrived back at the dorm before Persephone and Adonis returned? Too late, Persephone wished she'd left a note. Unfortunately, the magic breezes that delivered messages didn't come to the Underworld, so there was no way to contact her now.

A half hour later the cloth petals on the floppy yellow poppy began to flutter. Adonis had woken from his catnap. As Persephone went to check on him, the bag tipped over and he scooted out. Picking one of the asphodel flowers, she held it by its long stem and dangled the flower part so he could play bat-the-blossom.

All at once she heard a loud *honk* and the sound of wings flapping overhead. Looking up, she was astonished to see Aphrodite and her swan cart. *Uh-oh.* The swans glided smoothly, their long necks stretched out in front of them. They landed in the field not more than ten yards away.

Persephone scooped up Adonis as Aphrodite stepped from her cart. As soon as her feet touched the ground, the cart shrank into a figurine again. She picked it up, then slipped it into her pocket.

Spotting Persephone holding Adonis, Aphrodite frowned and stomped toward them. Persephone cuddled the kitten close. She knew Aphrodite was not going to be happy she'd brought the kitten down here. "How did you find me?" she asked.

"Pheme saw you from a window."

"Oh!" Persephone said. So that's who'd been watching her and Hades as they were leaving MOA.

"I came to get *my* kitten," Aphrodite announced. But before she could even try to snatch Adonis away, he leaped from Persephone's arms. Ignoring both girls, he romped merrily off among the asphodel stalks. Pausing a short distance away, he began to lick his paw.

They both went after him but then stopped to argue. "Did you think you could hide him from me here? Then maybe smuggle him to your mom's? Were you going to pretend he got lost and then keep him for yourself?" Aphrodite demanded.

Persephone stiffened. "What? Are you accusing me of kitten-napping Adonis?"

"Well, I don't recall giving you permission to bring him here," said Aphrodite.

"Hades needed me to come help him. It was an emergency," Persephone informed her. "You weren't back yet. I couldn't very well take Adonis to you at the track, or leave him alone in your room. What was I supposed to do?"

"Leave a note?"

Persephone threw her arms wide. "I forgot! So sue me in the courts of Athens! Don't try to push the blame on me. I was just trying to take care of Adonis. Someone had to!"

Eyes flashing, Aphrodite poked a pink-polished fingertip to her own chest. "*I* can take care of him!"

"I never said you couldn't," Persephone protested. Though, now that she thought about it, she'd certainly spent more time caring for the kitten than Aphrodite had. If Adonis were able to choose between them, she was sure he'd pick *her*!

"He's *mine*," Aphrodite said, as if reading Persephone's mind.

Persephone crossed her arms. "Tell Adonis that!" she shot back. "Maybe he'd rather belong to me!"

"I knew it! You *were* trying to steal him!" Aphrodite shouted. In a huff, she turned to get Adonis. But he wasn't there anymore. "Here kitty, kitty," she called to him. He didn't come.

"Oh, no!" Persephone exclaimed. She began to look around and call to him too. But to no avail. The girls had been arguing so hard that neither of them had kept an eye on the kitten. Now he had wandered off and was lost!

Fields of asphodel were perfectly harmless, but other parts of the Underworld could prove dangerous to a sweet, unsuspecting kitten. What if Adonis fell into a river of lava!

Persephone wrung her hands, wishing she'd never let Hades talk her into coming here. If Adonis got hurt, it would be all her fault!

15

Aphrodite

Friday afternoon.

FURIOUS WITH PERSEPHONE, APHRODITE SET her swan figurine on the ground and recited the chant to make it come to life. "I'll see if I can spot Adonis from overhead," she said, her voice tight.

"Let me help! Four eyes are better than two," Persephone pleaded.

Aphrodite hesitated. Part of her wanted to refuse Persephone's help and stay mad. But another part knew she should forgive her. After all, Persephone was just as worried about the kitten as *she* was. "Okay. Thanks." Truth was, she was grateful for the help.

As the swans' wings unfurled and began to flap, the two goddessgirls leaped into the cart. Soon they were soaring over the snowy-white fields of asphodel. Once, they thought they saw the kitten sitting near some shades who were hoeing a field. But when they dipped lower, they saw it was only a black rock.

Widening their search, they swept along the banks of the River Lethe. "What if Adonis was thirsty?" Aphrodite said, hearing the fear in her own voice. Those who drank from this river forgot everyone and everything they'd ever known. She wouldn't mind if the kitten forgot Persephone. But she wanted him to remember *her*!

"I gave him a drink earlier," said Persephone, sounding hopeful that he hadn't gone to the river. When they didn't see him there, they flew onward. Soon they were over the deep gloomy pit that was Tartarus. "There's Hades," Persephone murmured. "And those giants with him must be the Titans who tried to escape."

Hades appeared to be scolding them, shaking a finger in front of their faces. He was so into his lecture that he didn't even look up as the girls sped by overhead.

Next, the girls flew past a man chained to a rock in the middle of a pool. A tree loaded with perfect pears hung just over his head. But when he reached out hungrily to grab one, the branches of the tree lifted higher, so they were always beyond his grasp.

Persephone motioned to Aphrodite to fly on by. As the man scowled after them, Persephone explained. "He must have done something really bad. Those tempting, out-of-reach pears are his punishment."

"Oh. I see," said Aphrodite. Whatever he'd done must have been truly terrible, she thought, because those pears looked *tantalizingly* delicious! "I hope Adonis isn't out there somewhere, hungry too. Because *he* doesn't deserve to be punished!"

"I know. This is my fault. I shouldn't have brought him here," said Persephone. "I know it doesn't help, but I'm so sorry."

Aphrodite didn't answer. She'd wanted Persephone to admit she'd been wrong. But now that she had, Aphrodite didn't feel quite ready to forgive her. And that made her feel guilty, too. Which was ridonkulous! She'd done nothing wrong!

As the search dragged on, she began to despair. "What if we never find him," she wailed. Persephone grabbed her hand and gave it a comforting squeeze. She could always count on Persephone to try to make her feel better. Aphrodite's heart melted toward her just a teeny bit, even though she was still mad at her!

Leaving Tartarus, they sailed back over the asphodel fields again. As they neared the marsh at the entrance to the Underworld, they heard several dogs growling and snapping. Or maybe just one dog, Aphrodite decided. One *three-headed* dog that belonged to Hades.

The girls looked at each other in alarm. "Cerberus!" they exclaimed at the same time.

They zoomed toward the growly sounds. Aphrodite was sure that she and Persephone were both picturing the same thing: Adonis being gobbled to bits. Never a dog fan to begin with, Aphrodite shuddered as she imagined Cerberus's slobbering jaws and sharp fangs. Suddenly the growling stopped.

185

"Oh, no!" she whispered, freaking out. The terrible, empty silence was even *scarier* than the growling had been!

"What if . . . ?" Persephone began, but she couldn't finish. Tears filled her eyes. This time it was Aphrodite who gave *her* hand a comforting squeeze.

If only Adonis was okay, she'd try to be a nicer person, Aphrodite silently promised herself. She'd stop being mad at Persephone. She'd . . . she'd do anything! If only the kitten was okay.

Spotting the dog below on the bank of the River Styx, she zoomed the swan cart in for a landing. The second it touched ground, she dashed off, not even waiting for the cart to shrink back into a figurine. Fortunately, Persephone stayed behind long enough to pocket it.

The swampy ground sucked at Aphrodite's sandals as

she rushed toward the dastardly three-headed dog, who'd found a dry spot of ground to rest upon. "What did you do with him?" she shouted. All three of Cerberus's heads swung her way. They growled in unison.

"Shh, Cerberus," Persephone called from somewhere behind her. "It's me, boy." Recognizing her voice, the dog wagged his long tail.

Just then Aphrodite spied a much smaller, cuter black tail poking up from between the dog's two enormous paws. She pointed at it, thinking the worst. "No-ooo. Adonis's tail!" she wailed. Cerberus shifted uncertainly, upset by her shouts.

All at once a kitten's head popped up from between the dog's paws. Green eyes blinked at them as if to say, *What's all the fuss?*

Aphrodite pointed, shouting, "Look! Adonis! He's okay!"

"Thank godness!" Persephone said, relief in her voice.

Unharmed, he was snuggled between Cerebus's paws. As they watched, Adonis wriggled around until he lay upside down, showing his white belly. All four of his precious little paws stretched up into the air.

One of the dog's heads bent down. It moved closer . . . and closer to the kitten. His mouth opened.

"No!" shrieked Aphrodite. "Don't you *dare* eat him!"

Ignoring her, Cerberus flicked out his big pink tongue . . . and gave the kitten a gentle lick. Adonis batted playfully at him with his paws. Then he leaped up. Nimbly, he scampered up the long nose of one dog head and down its long neck. Then he ran across the huge dog's back to the tip of its tail. Cerberus wriggled as if being tickled.

Rushing forward, Aphrodite scooped Adonis up. "Oh, you little cutie-pie! I was so worried about you!" she exclaimed, cuddling the kitten to her chest.

Persephone reached over to scratch Cerberus's back. "What a good dog you are for taking care of Adonis!" she told him.

In keeping with her silent promise, Aphrodite decided to stop blaming Persephone for what had happened. Yes, she shouldn't have taken the kitten to the Underworld. But they were *both* at fault for not keeping a better eye on him. Still, she didn't want to talk about that right now. She was too busy being thrilled over the fact that Adonis was okay!

As she cooed over him and stroked his sweet fur, she thought of another promise—the one she'd made to Athena to talk to Principal Zeus about keeping the kitten.

Well, she hadn't said *when* she'd talk to him. And it wouldn't be anytime soon. Because what if he told her Adonis had to go? No . . . she wouldn't think like that. Zeus just *had* to let her keep him!

16

Athena

Still Friday afternoon.

MEANWHILE, ATHENA WAS ANXIOUSLY searching the skies of Mount Olympus and beyond for Pegasus and Bellerophon as she and Artemis sailed eastward in the deer-drawn chariot. Her hopes rose when she spotted something off in the distance winging its way toward them.

Was it Pegasus? she wondered excitedly. Pointing, she called, "Look! Over there." But as Artemis's chariot drew closer, Athena's heart sank. The winged thing turned out to be Hermes in his delivery chariot. He waved to them as he continued on his rounds, delivering packages.

Minutes later her hopes were boosted again when she spied another winged figure. Only, this time it turned out to be a harpy—a winged bird-woman. With a shriek it swooped toward their chariot in search of food to snatch, but the girls shooed it away.

"I think we should turn back," Athena suggested reluctantly. "Just because Pegasus and Bellerophon started out going east, they might not have continued in the same direction."

Artemis must've been thinking the same thing because she nodded. "Yeah. They could've circled around before we even started out. Maybe they're already back at MOA."

Athena nodded, but she didn't want to get her hopes up only to have them dashed again. Where could they be? She was mad and worried at the same time. Mad that Bellerophon had ridden Pegasus so far away, leaving her to face Zeus's possible—no, *probable*—wrath. And worried that something might've happened to them.

Artemis called to her deer, and soon the chariot was circling back. They were nearing MOA when a dense layer of dark gray clouds formed behind them. Winds whipped up, knocking the chariot from side to side.

"This is bad," Artemis groaned. "I haven't seen angry clouds like these since before Zeus met Hera, when he was all lonely and in a bad mood."

"Do you think this is my dad's doing?" Athena had to shout to be heard over the wind. "Like maybe he's mad because he found out about Bellerophon and Pegasus?"

"All I know is that if this storm hangs around through tomorrow, the Games will be rained out!" Artemis shouted back.

She looked really upset. Realizing she was struggling for control of the chariot, Athena grabbed the reins to assist. As they fought to keep from crashing, something enormous burst through the clouds right behind them. It was strange and terrifying. And it had killer bad breath.

Artemis gasped. "Ye gods! A *Chimera*!"

"W-what?" Athena sputtered, freaking out at this news. "Are you sure?"

"Yes!" said Artemis, glancing over her shoulder as the monster gave chase. "Beast-ology is my best subject, remember?"

Sure enough, the creature did have a lion's head in front, a fire-breathing goat's head in back, and a serpent tail. Artemis was right!

"But I thought the Chimera only made trouble in the mountains and forests of—" Athena stopped, realizing what she'd been about to say. *Lycia*. A kingdom far to the southeast of Mount Olympus and across the sea. It was the king of Lycia who'd been visiting Zeus when she and Bellerophon tried to see him this morning!

She remembered what Zeus had said: "Thunderation! You say it may be coming this way?" No wonder he'd been worried. And no wonder Ms. Hydra had predicted disaster for MOA. The king of Lycia must've been warning Zeus about the monster's approach!

Mega-bad storms always followed in the Chimera's wake. If it attacked MOA, who knew what terrors might follow? There wasn't time to tell Artemis any of this.

Which was just as well. If that girl had one more thing to worry about regarding the Games, her head might explode.

"It's gaining on us!" Artemis yelled.

Closer now, the beast's serpentine tail thrashed about, snapping in the air like a whip. Its lion head gave a mighty roar.

"Watch out!" Athena shouted as flames shot from its mouth.

"Dive!" Artemis told her deer. They plunged downward in the nick of time and the flames sailed harmlessly over the top of the chariot.

But the Chimera wasn't giving up. It dove too. Probably it was anticipating a dinner of deer meat and goddessgirls! Catching up to them, it roared again. A fireball of bad breath and flames burst from its goat throat this time.

Artemis's deer veered left. Athena felt the heat as the stinky fireball shot by. It missed them by mere inches. *P.U.!*

Artemis reached over her shoulder as if to grab an arrow from her quiver. "Oh, no," she moaned. "I left my bow and arrows back in the gym!"

The chariot jerked this way and that like a storm-tossed ship as the panicked deer zigzagged first one way and then another to avoid the Chimera's wrath. Though they were agile and quick, they were tiring. They were no match for this fiendish monster!

Terrified, Athena couldn't take her eyes from it. What if Pegasus and Bellerophon had met up with this Chimera too? She shuddered to think that by granting Bellerophon's wish, she might have doomed them all.

The Chimera roared again, and another fireball blasted from it. Again, Athena felt its heat. She thought they had dodged it, though. That is, until Artemis yelled, "The chariot's on fire!"

Ripping a wide swatch of cloth from the hem of her chiton, Athena beat at the flames and managed to smother them. But now the Chimera was nearly upon them. She braced for another fireball.

Just then, from high above them, she heard the beating of wings. She looked up. "Pegasus!"

With Bellerophon astride him, the winged horse parted the clouds and swooped directly at the monster. Athena tried to wave them off. "No! You'll be fried!"

But at the last possible second Bellerophon leaped from Pegasus to straddle the Chimera's back and Pegasus zoomed away. When the startled lion's head opened its mouth to let out yet another roar, Bellerophon wrapped his arms around its throat in a choke hold. Smoke shot out of the monster's ears.

"I think a fireball got trapped in its throat," Athena told Artemis.

"Couldn't happen to a meaner monster!" Artemis gloated in satisfaction.

As they watched, the Chimera's eyes bugged out and its tail drooped. Still, Bellerophon kept his arms firmly locked around the creature's neck. Athena could see he was tiring, though. What if he couldn't finish the job? The Chimera might finish them off instead!

Thinking fast, she leaned over the side of the chariot, calling out to the beast. "Hey, you—Chimera! If you'll agree to let me put a banishment spell on you, we'll let you go."

The monster's lion head and goat head looked at her and then at each other. Then they both nodded desperately. Wasting no time, Athena recited a spell, which would only work when a beast agreed to it first.

"From Mount Olympus,

I thee banish.

Go, Chimera—

vamoose, vanish!"

"All right!" Bellerophon shouted in victory when she finished. Immediately, he let go of the Chimera's neck. It shook its head and coughed out a series of smoke rings.

All this time Pegasus had been hovering overhead. Now he swooped lower. Reaching up, Bellerophon caught hold of the golden bridle and leaped onto Pegasus's back. "See you at the Academy!" he called to the girls. Then he shouted, "Yaaah-hooo!"

As he and Pegasus winged away, a subdued-looking Chimera flapped in the opposite direction, toward Lycia. Fortunately, the dark clouds went with it. As the clouds lifted, the sun began to shine again. Athena and Artemis looked at each other and smiled.

"Phew! That was quick thinking," Artemis told her admiringly.

"Thanks," said Athena. Zeus was going to be pleased to know that the Chimera was no longer a threat to MOA. She only hoped he didn't find out about the rest of this fiasco, though!

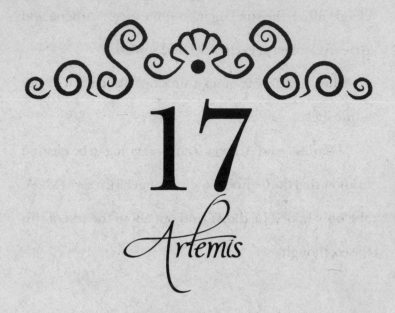

17

Artemis

Friday, early evening.

As soon as Artemis and Athena entered the Academy, Artemis headed for the marble staircase that led to the dorms. "I'll take my dogs out and meet you in the cafeteria in a few," she told Athena.

"Okay," Athena replied.

Artemis raced upstairs. When she opened her door,

her dogs immediately crowded around her. They sniffed her all over. Had some of the Chimera's stinky breath stuck to her? Or were they just smelling her deer? Hard to say. "Come on, boys. I'll take you outside," she told them.

It couldn't have been more than fifteen minutes later when she and her dogs joined Athena at the goddessgirls' usual table. Yet news about the Chimera had already started to spread. "Did you hear?" Pheme said, rushing up to them. "The Chimera tried to wage an attack on MOA!"

"Oh, no!" said Athena, faking surprise.

"Oh, yes!" said Pheme. Then she dashed off, running from table to table. Naturally, she was delighted to have a new story to pass around.

"That Bellyache—" Artemis huffed.

"Bellerophon," Athena corrected.

"Uh-huh," said Artemis. "Well, he has a big mouth. He should've known better than to brag about his adventures with a horse he practically stole from Principal Zeus." She looked around but didn't see the boy anywhere. "Lucky for him, he's not here. Or else he'd get a piece of my mind!"

She dreaded to think what would happen if the Chimera tale reached Zeus's ears. He'd be glad to know that the Chimera had been banished, of course. But if he found out that she and Athena had been involved . . . well . . . it was pretty much a Zeus-aster waiting to happen.

Aphrodite and Persephone soon joined them for dinner. As the four goddessgirls ate, they chatted about all that had gone on that day. Artemis noticed that the tension between Aphrodite and Persephone seemed to have eased. Maybe their scare over almost losing

Adonis in the Underworld had knocked some sense into them!

She also noticed that Aphrodite's floppy poppy bag was sitting on a chair between the two of them. And it was wriggling. "Adonis? Are you crazy?" she said. Until the bag began to move, her dogs had quietly lain at her feet. But now they lifted their ears and sat up. "Stay," she commanded. Luckily, they obeyed.

Athena shook her head. "Yeah, I can't believe you'd risk bringing that kitten here again."

"After all he's been through, we couldn't just leave him alone in the dorm," said Persephone. She sneaked a bit of fish from her plate into the bag.

"And we were so traumatized at losing him that now we can't bear to let him out of our sight," Aphrodite added in her usual dramatic way. She stuck her hand in the bag to pet the kitten.

Persephone nudged her with an elbow. "Show them the collar Hephaestus made." Hephaestus, who also attended MOA, was the godboy of blacksmiths and metalworking. He could craft the most beautiful things from gold, silver, and gemstones.

Eyes sparkling, Aphrodite drew a jeweled collar from the pocket of her chiton. "It's for Adonis," she said as she passed the collar to Athena. "I haven't even had time to put it on him yet. Hephaestus just finished it."

"Ooh! Pretty," said Athena. Artemis also leaned in to look. It *was* pretty! Maybe she should get Hephaestus to make collars for her dogs too.

"The windflower design was my idea," Persephone said proudly. The colorful "flowers" were gold-linked together like a daisy chain. Each flower was made up of jeweled petals around an amber center. And hanging from the middle of the collar was a tiny golden bell.

Artemis reached out and flicked it, and it made a cheerful tinkling sound.

"The bell was my idea," Aphrodite explained. "So we'll be able to hear Adonis if he ever wanders away from us again."

Artemis noticed she was saying "we" and "us" instead of "me." She and Persephone were definitely getting along better. Just then, out of the corner of her eye, Artemis happened to notice Pheme standing near the cafeteria door. She was staring their way, and she looked kind of . . . shocked.

"Quick, Pheme's watching. Hide the collar," she whispered.

Aphrodite hurriedly stuck it back in her pocket.

"Where? I don't see her," Persephone said, looking around.

Artemis glanced over again, but Pheme had gone.

"Well, she *was* here and I think she saw the collar. If she asks, let's all say it's a dog collar for Suez. Anyway, I thought we were all trying to keep Adonis a secret. But now Hades and Hephaestus know too."

Aphrodite frowned. "Two more people. That's not so many."

"Besides, Aphrodite's going to tell my dad soon anyway. Right?" Athena hinted. Aphrodite quickly changed the subject, and fifteen minutes later lunch was over.

They were just getting ready to leave when a hush fell over the entire cafeteria. The kind of hush that usually occurred when . . . *Uh-oh!*

Artemis looked up. Sure enough, Zeus was looming in the doorway, scanning the students. Everyone ducked or looked away, probably hoping his thunderous gaze wouldn't settle on them. Suddenly his arm rose from his side. His finger pointed across the room. At *their* table!

"YOU FOUR!" his voice boomed. "THEENY . . . APHRODITE . . . PERSEPHONE . . . ARTEMIS! GET TO MY OFFICE. *NOW!*" Then he swung his arm around and pointed in the direction of his office. As if they didn't know where it was.

The four goddessgirls exchanged worried glances as they jumped up from their seats. Artemis's eyes fell on the ugly floppy poppy bag as Aphrodite picked it up. They couldn't just leave it here with Adonis inside, of course. So Adonis would have to come with them. This was going to be bad.

All eyes were on the girls as they picked their way toward the exit. Artemis's hounds trotted along behind her, obediently ignoring the bag Aphrodite was carrying.

After they exited the cafeteria, Artemis noticed Aphrodite edging toward the stairs that led to the dorms. She was obviously hoping to sneak up to her room and drop off Adonis.

"You!" Zeus thundered at her before she could escape. "No detours." Then he headed down the hall for his office. The girls followed, of course. Including Aphrodite. No one dared disobey.

It wasn't fair, Artemis moped. Why was *she* in trouble? The Bellerophon thing wasn't her fault, if that's what Zeus was mad about. Well, she supposed it was true that she hadn't gotten permission to fly her chariot as far as she had when she'd helped Athena go after Bellerophon and Pegasus.

But if they hadn't, the Chimera might've destroyed the Academy! So really, they'd done the whole school a favor. She hoped Zeus would see it that way. She crossed her fingers that he wasn't mad enough to cancel the Games.

Principal Zeus halted in the doorway of his office, waiting. As they all tromped past, he pointed to some chairs lined up in front of his desk. "SIT!" he said sternly. Immediately Artemis's dogs plopped their bottoms down on the floor in the middle of the doorway. They looked alertly up at him as if awaiting his next command.

"He didn't mean you," Artemis whispered, nudging them to move. "C'mon." The middle chair in the row facing Zeus's desk was already occupied. By Bellerophon. Artemis and Athena made *yikes* faces at each other. Since Bellerophon was here, that must mean Principal Zeus already knew about Pegasus being "borrowed" without his permission. This was going to be *stupendously* bad.

Persephone and Aphrodite sat on one side of Bellerophon, Athena on the other side. Artemis started to sit by Athena, but seeing something on the chair seat, she picked it up. It was a tube of lip gloss. *Orange* lip gloss. Pheme had been here! Spreading gossip, no doubt. Artemis set the tube on the edge of Zeus's desk, then sat. Her dogs settled at her feet.

Zeus plunked down on the golden throne behind his desk, not seeming to notice the tube. But she knew that all her friends had seen it, and they'd realize exactly who'd been bending his ear with gossip. One of these days, all that gossip was going to turn around and bite Pheme on the patoot!

Elbows on his desk, Zeus steepled his hands together. Artemis held her breath as he opened his mouth to speak.

Only instead of speaking, he scrunched up his face in a funny way. And then, he . . . sneezed. "Ah-ah-ah-CHOOO!" The sneeze was so strong, it blew his office door shut with a *bang.* All five kids jumped.

Athena looked at him anxiously. "Are you catching a cold, Dad?"

Zeus's thick reddish brows rammed together. "Of course not. I'm never sick. As King of the Gods and Ruler of the Heavens, I don't have *time* to be sick!" He paused. "And do you know what else I don't have time for?" His piercing blue eyes pinned his five victims to their chairs.

"What?" squeaked Artemis when no one else answered.

"RULE BREAKERS!" Zeus thumped his desk with a fist. Tiny thunderbolts shot out from between his knuckles making scorch marks on the wall to the right of his desk.

"We're sorry," Athena said, shifting nervously. "We didn't mean to break any rules." The others nodded.

"Uh . . . what rules did we break?" Artemis dared to ask. Because she really didn't know—*none* of them knew—what Zeus had found out. Exactly what was he so mega mad about? Was it the Pegasus-stealing? The Chimera-battling? Or the kitten-keeping? They'd been breaking a lot of rules lately.

Zeus looked about to speak, but then his face scrunched up again. "Ah-ah-ah-CHOO!" Whipping a monogrammed handkerchief from his desk drawer, he blew his nose with a loud *honk*. Immediately he was attacked by another series of sneezes.

Trying to communicate without words, he began flapping his arms like wings. Then he flicked his head in a way that reminded her of a horse. "NEIGH-CHOO!" he sneezed.

"Is this about Pegasus?" Artemis guessed when nobody else made a peep. Seriously, they'd be here all day if no one spoke up.

"EGG-GG-XACTLY!" Zeus spoke-sneezed. Bellerophon and Athena shrank lower in their chairs. "No one rides him without *my* permission," Zeus went on. "And especially not to fight the Chimera!" He eyed Athena as he pointed at Bellerophon. "This boy could've gotten . . . gotten . . ." For a few seconds he seemed to hang on the brink of another humongous sneeze.

"Fried? Crunched? Mangled?" Artemis blurted out possible endings for Zeus's sentence as the others sat mute. But each time, Zeus shook his head. "Killed?" she tried finally.

"RIGHT-CHOOO-ARRR," Zeus managed to sneeze-speak. He spread his arms wide. "Now tell me, is *that* the way we treat guests at MOA?"

"No," Athena admitted. "But all's well that ends well, right? Bellerophon's fine and the Chimera's gone." Having finally found her tongue, she went on to tell him about the similar dreams she and Bellerophon had had. Zeus listened intently.

"I wonder, Dad. Are you sure you didn't put the idea of the golden bridle into our heads?" she asked at the end of her story. "You probably knew that Bellerophon could succeed in turning the Chimera away with Pegasus's help. Right?"

Artemis caught Athena's eye and grinned. Athena wasn't the goddessgirl of wisdom for nothing. Everyone knew that Zeus liked to take credit for good ideas.

Zeus stroked his bushy red beard as if considering what Athena had said. "I might've done that," he said with a tentative smile. "It sounds like something I might do." His smile widened. "In fact, the more I think about it, the more I'm sure that's *exactly* what I did. It's too good an idea for me *not* to have thought of it!"

After another sneezing fit, Zeus excused Bellerophon. The boy leaped up in obvious relief and ran out the door.

Phew, thought Artemis. Looked like tomorrow's Games weren't doomed to be canceled after all! She stood, thinking they'd all been excused.

"SIT! STAY!" shouted Zeus.

Artemis sat. Her dogs stayed.

Zeus's sneezing calmed momentarily. "There's another matter we need to discuss," he said, sounding serious. His gaze swung to Aphrodite and Persephone. The two of them had been sitting quietly. Probably hoping to escape his notice. The floppy poppy bag was between them, and each girl held one of its handles.

"It's easy to be drawn to pretty things," Zeus began kindly. "Especially if you're the goddessgirl of beauty," he said, looking at Aphrodite. "Or the goddessgirl of lovely things like flowers," he said, switching his gaze to Persephone. "But I can't allow the two of you to keep it."

"Oh, please," said Aphrodite. Her fingers tightened on the bag's strap.

"We know it was wrong not to tell you," Persephone added.

"But I promise I'll take good care of—" Aphrodite and Persephone said at the same time. Then they glared at each other.

Hmm, thought Artemis, maybe things *weren't* so smooth between those two yet, after all.

"STOP!" roared Zeus at last. "I cannot allow theft."

Theft? All four goddessgirls stared at him, stunned.

"But I *found* him," Aphrodite said. "He was abandoned." She lifted the woven bag into her lap and wrapped her arms around it, kitten and all. She looked ready to cry. So did Persephone.

"Is that the . . . ah-ah-ah-CHOO! . . . necklace?" Zeus asked.

"Necklace?" the girls all echoed in confusion.

Suddenly Artemis guessed what was going on. "You mean Freya's necklace?" she asked. "You think they stole it?"

"I have it on good authority that you've all been hiding something."

Hmpf, thought Artemis. Her eyes went to the lip gloss on the desk. Since when was Pheme a "good authority"? How could she—how could Zeus—think that her friends would steal Freya's necklace?

"We would never—" Persephone started to say.

"Not in a hundred—" Aphrodite interrupted.

Artemis snapped her fingers as she realized what must've happened. "Back in the cafeteria today— remember when I thought Pheme saw the collar?" she told the other girls. "She must've thought it was Freya's necklace!"

"That rat!" said Aphrodite. She drew the collar from her pocket. Hefting the straps of her bag over one shoulder, she left her chair to show the collar to Zeus. "This is what Pheme saw. Hephaestus made it for Adonis."

Zeus studied the jeweled collar, sneezing all the while. "Ah-choo! Ah-choo. Ah-WHO?"

"Adonis," Artemis repeated for him. "I hope you haven't developed an allergy to my dogs," she added worriedly.

Zeus shook his head, handing the collar back. "The only thing I'm allergic to is—" Just then Adonis stuck his head out of Aphrodite's bag. Pushing off, he jumped smack in the middle of Zeus's desk. *"CATS!"* Zeus finished, his eyes wide. Then he let out a whopping sneeze, followed quickly by five more.

Looks like the cat's finally out of the bag, thought Artemis. *Literally!*

Before they could stop him, Adonis leaped onto Zeus's broad chest, grasping his tunic with his claws.

The goddessgirls exchanged horrified looks as Principal Zeus pointed at the door. "Get this cat OUT-*CHOOOOOO!*"

18

Persephone

Friday evening.

THE SOUND OF PRINCIPAL ZEUS'S SNEEZES echoed down the halls of MOA and followed the four goddessgirls all the way upstairs to their dorm. "He didn't say Adonis had to leave MOA, just his office, right?" Aphrodite asked anxiously. After helping unhook Adonis's claws from Zeus's tunic, she'd scooped the kitten up and fled the office. Now he was cuddled close to her chest.

"Right," Persephone agreed. She was worried, though. Some people were allergic to flowers, too, and couldn't be around them. How could they keep a cat at the Academy if their principal was allergic?

Artemis had almost reached her door when she stopped in the middle of the hallway and smacked a hand to her forehead. "Godsamighty!" she exclaimed. "The new archery targets still need to be unpacked and set up. Tonight!" She groaned.

"I'll help," Persephone offered.

"Me too," added Athena.

"Count me in," said Aphrodite. "Oh, wait. Guess I'd better stay behind and keep Adonis company."

Persephone looked longingly at the kitten. She'd rather stay too. After the wild day Adonis had had, he

223

needed reassurance. Who better to give it than *her*? And what if Zeus announced in the morning that Adonis had to leave MOA? Tonight might be all the time they had with him. Sadness filled her at the very idea. Still, it wasn't fair to make Artemis do all the work.

"You guys don't have to help," Artemis said, seeming to sense her reluctance. "I can manage."

"I'm sure you can," said Persephone. "But that's not the point. We're in the Girl Games together." She glanced at Athena. "We *want* to help, right?"

Athena nodded at Artemis. "Definitely. Besides, if I hadn't nabbed you from the gym to look for Pegasus and Bellerophon, those targets would already be unpacked."

"All right, then. Thanks," said Artemis, looking relieved. She shooed her dogs into her room and quickly fed them. Then she, Persephone, and Athena all headed off together.

Outside, Persephone inhaled the scent of flowers in the air and looked up at the star-filled sky. "What a nice night," she said.

Bunches of students were hanging out in the courtyard, including Apollo, Hades, and Actaeon. She waved to them, but the boys didn't notice because Penthe walked up to them just then. Glancing at Artemis, Persephone saw that she was watching Penthe too.

Artemis's eyes narrowed as the Amazon girl tapped Actaeon on the shoulder. She said something to him and then laughed in a flirty way. Actaeon shrugged and said something in reply.

"Well, it *was* a nice night," Artemis muttered in a tight voice.

Persephone linked arms with both her friends and steered them onward. "It's always nice when we're hanging out together," she said gently. Athena agreed.

Artemis sent Persephone a small, grateful smile. Still, Persephone understood her mood. If Penthe tried to flirt with Hades, *she'd* be upset too!

The boxes of new targets were still sitting in a corner of the storage room when the three goddessgirls arrived at the gym. They tore them open and checked that all twenty targets had arrived.

"Fancy Flyers?" Athena asked, reading the label on the back of a target she'd just unpacked.

Artemis shrugged. "It's just the name of the company that makes them."

"Ha! I was hoping the targets really *would* fly," joked Persephone. "How fun would that be?"

Artemis grinned. "Well, it would be *different* anyway!"

Together, the girls lugged the targets out to the

archery range. It was dark now, but there were torch-lights around the perimeter of the empty field. "Every-one must be resting up for tomorrow's competitions," said Athena, looking around.

"Like we should be," said Artemis. "Let's get this done."

"There sure is a lot of set-up work before an Olympics," Athena commented as they took down the old, battered targets and replaced them with the new un-holey ones.

"Tell me about it," Artemis said under her breath, but her friends overheard.

"I'm sorry," Athena said. "I should've been helping more."

"Me too," said Persephone. She'd offered, but Artemis had always refused, acting like she wanted to control everything to do with the Games. Persephone wondered if Artemis just hadn't known it was okay to need help once in a while.

"Not your fault," Artemis admitted now. "I guess I shouldn't have tried to do it all myself." With three of them to do the work, it didn't take long. Still, it was way past dark by the time they started back to MOA and climbed the stairs to the dorm.

"Night!" Persephone called to the other two as they all went to their rooms.

Artemis yawned. "Night."

"Good luck to all of us tomorrow," Athena called softly.

"Yes to that!" Persephone called back, keeping her voice low so as not to wake anyone.

Aphrodite was already in bed asleep when she entered the room. Adonis lay beside her in the crook of her arm. Persephone resisted the urge to pick him up and move him to *her* bed. Instead, she changed into her pj's. And after a quick trip down the hall to brush her teeth, she slipped under her covers and fell fast asleep.

Saturday morning.

When Persephone woke, Adonis was curled up next to her on the bed. Aphrodite was already dressed in the sparkly pink running outfit she'd bought at the Immortal Marketplace.

Persephone raised up on her elbows, pushing her long wavy red hair out of her face. "Happy Girl Games Day!" she told Aphrodite. "You look nice."

Aphrodite looked over and smiled. "Happy Girl Games Day to you too. And thanks for the compliment. I may not win the race, but I plan to look good trying!"

Persephone laughed. Sitting up, she pulled the kitten onto her lap and began to pet it. Neither she nor

Aphrodite spoke about Zeus and their worry that he might banish Adonis. Persephone just wanted to hold on to hope for as long as she could. She figured Aphrodite felt the same way.

Someone knocked on the door. "You awake in there?" Athena whispered from the hall.

"Come in!" Aphrodite called.

The door opened and Athena and Artemis came in. Athena was wearing her navy-blue running chiton, and Artemis had on a stretchy crimson one.

Artemis smiled broadly and spread her arms. "It's the Girl Games! Finally. Can you believe it?"

Suddenly all four goddessgirls had linked arms and were jumping around in an excited group hug. "Woohoo! Yay! Girls *rock*!"

After they'd calmed down, Artemis said, "I'm starving. Let's go eat."

Persephone put on a perky yellow-and-white-striped chiton her mother had sewn especially for the Games, then the four girls went downstairs to the cafeteria. They were all too revved up to eat much breakfast and were soon on their way to the sports fields together.

There was no need to hide the kitten anymore since Principal Zeus already knew about him. So Aphrodite brought Adonis, holding him in her arms. Every now and then Persephone reached over and petted his soft fur.

Other students paused to ask about the kitten and coo over him. Adonis didn't seem scared at all. He just licked everyone and turned his head this way and that, as if interested in everything. *He was the best, bravest, cutest kitten ever!* thought Persephone.

Up ahead, colorful banners and flags fluttered atop the tall poles that lined the sports fields and the track.

The banners were decorated with symbols for each sport in the Girl Games.

"Wow," Artemis said admiringly. "Hera really came through with the decorations!"

Athena smiled. "She had some help. The seamstresses at her wedding shop made them."

"Yeah, sometimes asking for help is a *good* thing," Persephone said, giving Artemis a pointed look.

Artemis smiled a little sheepishly. "Okay, I get it. But I just wanted things to be perfect."

"And they are," said Aphrodite, her blue eyes sparkling. "The stands are packed. Everyone's excited. Look how awesome this is!"

Horns blared and the girls rushed to find seats together. Soon afterward the heralds announced the official start of the girls' very first Olympics. *Ta-ta-ta-TAH!* They each blew on a salpinx, a long, thin, trumpetlike instrument that ended in a curved bell.

A humongous cheer went up from the crowd as bluebirds flew overhead forming a giant "HG" logo, which stood for the Heraean Games. Then confetti exploded from the few puffy clouds in the sky, swirling down upon them all in colorful whirls.

In unison, the heralds announced the schedule of the day's events. The long jump was first, so Persephone leaped from her seat and zipped onto the field below.

After she and her competitors were all gathered together, they drew numbers to determine the jumping order. Each of them would get two jumps total.

When Persephone read the number on the papyrus slip she'd drawn, she glanced at the other three goddessgirls watching from the stands. *Last,* she mouthed.

"Good luck!" "Rock it!" she heard them call back.

She sort of wished she'd drawn an early slot. Then she could've gotten her jumps over with right away. But she smiled and waved, grateful for her friends' support.

She met Hades at the special competition pit that had been constructed at the track's center. "You ready for this?" he asked as she began her warm-up exercises.

"Ready as I'll ever be," she replied nervously.

"Just remember everything I taught you and you'll be fine," he told her.

Easy for you to say, Persephone almost shot back. There were just so many of his instructions to keep in mind!

She didn't watch the other jumpers. It would only make her more stressed if she knew what distance she'd have to top to win. Better to just do her best and not think about anyone else. Still, though she turned her back on the pit, she couldn't help hearing the cheers of the crowd when one of the girls jumped especially far.

When it was finally her turn, Persephone took her place a proper distance from the pit. Her hands and knees shook just thinking about everyone watching her. *Stop it,* she told herself. *Ignore them.*

Hades' instructions ran through her head. *Focus. Rhythm. Hit the board in just the right place. Don't tense. Cycle forward.* It made her brain hurt just trying to remember them all.

Then she was off and running. She knew she was in trouble right away. Her rhythm was uneven. Afraid of overstepping the foul line, she started her jump too early.

She landed short. Magical pink sand shot up in the air to form the numbers thirteen and six.

Persephone groaned. *Thirteen feet, six inches?* Even without knowing the other girls' distances, she knew it wasn't good enough. Not by a long shot.

Hades sent her an encouraging smile as she brushed off the sand and walked back to begin her second and final jump. If she'd disappointed him, he was doing his best not to show it. When she reached her starting spot again, she glanced up in the stands at her friends.

Aphrodite caught her eye. Holding the kitten up, she yelled, "Do it for Adonis!"

Persephone grinned. Just seeing Adonis sent a wave of happiness through her. And the silly idea of jumping to please a kitten actually made her relax. She glanced over at Hades again. He gave her a thumbs-up.

For some reason, the pomegranate-seed-spitting contest they'd had when she was first getting to know him flashed through her mind. Seed spitting was something she was really, really good at. She could send a seed flying farther than anyone she knew.

Closing her eyes, she pictured herself as a seed sailing

through the air. *Yes,* she thought. *That's it. I'll be like a seed!*

This time when she sprinted toward the board, she didn't think about what her arms and legs were doing. She just ran. As soon as she lifted off from the board, she knew it was going to be a good jump. She could just *feel* it.

Time seemed to slow as she eyed the place where she wanted to land. *I'm a seed, I'm a seed riding the wind,* she thought.

Soaring farther than she'd ever gone before, she cycled her arms and legs forward to get every last inch out of her jump. As her heels hit the sand, her knees gave a little, just the way they were supposed to, and her hips carried her forward. The crowd whooped with excitement as the sparkly pink sand swirled around her.

When the numbers formed in the air, Persephone couldn't believe it. *Seventeen, three.* Her longest jump ever! It was a jump she could be proud of, regardless of whether or not she'd won.

As the crowd continued to cheer, she brushed herself off and stepped out of the pit. Suddenly Hades was lifting her high in the air and twirling her around.

"Not bad, huh?" she said breathlessly after he set her back down.

"You were awesome!" he said.

"So, who won?" she asked.

He stared at her in surprise. "You did, you nut. Didn't you know?"

She stared back at him. "Really? Leaping Olympians!" Impulsively, she leaned forward and kissed him on the cheek.

"Whoa," he said, blushing. But under the blush he was grinning from ear to ear. Just then Hera approached. Since Zeus had officially named these Games in her honor, it was she who would crown the champions with the traditional olive wreath.

"That was a terrific jump," said Hera. After placing the very first wreath of the Games on top of Persephone's head, she shook her hand. "Congratulations."

"Thank you." Persephone waved at the crowd as they applauded and whistled. Only now did she allow herself to think about the prizes she had won. As a champion, she'd have no homework for a whole month. And she'd get an Immortal Marketplace shopping certificate.

Best of all, a statue inscribed with her name would be erected in one of Hera's temples on Earth. Or if she didn't want a statue, she could choose to have a painted portrait of herself placed on a temple column. Incredible!

Persephone practically floated over to the stands where she accepted more congratulations and hugs from her friends. Then Aphrodite put Adonis into

Persephone's arms. "Take care of him," she said just before she, Athena, and Artemis hurried to the track. Their footrace would start next.

"I will," Persephone said softly after Aphrodite had gone. She hugged the kitten gently, practically melting when his round green eyes gazed up at her. Adonis rubbed his face against her cheek, purring. And right then she knew she'd give up all the prizes she'd won, if only Adonis could be hers forever.

19

Aphrodite

Saturday morning.

ARES WAS WAITING FOR APHRODITE alongside the track. It was only minutes before the two-hundred-meter race. "Now remember," he said. "Push out fast, pump with your arms, knees high, and take long strides. Don't worry about how you look."

It was all stuff he'd told her before, of course. "Do

you like my new running chiton?" she asked, twirling around in her sparkly pink outfit.

He frowned. "Uh-huh. Very nice."

"Oh, don't be so serious," Aphrodite said, playfully tapping his shoulder. "This is meant to be fun, right? That's why the events are called *games*."

Ares relaxed a little. "Right." Reaching out, he brushed back a strand of golden hair that had escaped her ponytail. His blue eyes softened as they looked down into hers. "But you *will* try to win, won't you?"

Aphrodite smiled. "You bet, godboy. I don't *do* losing," she said with a dramatic flourish.

"That's it. Think positive." Ares encouraged. "And remember the battle plan."

"Right. *Battle plan*," she said, smiling slightly. Who else but the godboy of war would think of a race as a battle?

Aphrodite felt curiously light and relaxed as she took her place on the girls' track. She stretched her legs as she waited for the race to begin.

She'd told Ares she didn't do losing. But really all she wanted was to enjoy the wonder of this moment. Just being here on the track in the very first Girl Games, with her friends all around her, was reward enough. It had taken a lot of planning for this to happen, and it would all be over way too soon.

Glancing several lanes over at Artemis and Athena, she smiled and waved. Athena returned her smile, but her expression was kind of tight. Did this race matter more to her brainy friend than she'd let on? Then again, maybe she was just upset that Heracles hadn't yet returned to MOA and so wasn't here for her race.

Artemis didn't even notice Aphrodite's friendly wave. She was staring straight ahead with the same fierce look of determination on her face that she always wore during any competition. Looking up into the stands, Aphrodite checked on Adonis and Persephone. Persephone held Adonis's paw up, moving it from side to side in a tiny wave. If she was secretly rooting for one of her three goddessgirl pals, she'd be too tactful to ever say.

A hush settled over the stands as the heralds blew on their salpinxes and announced the names of the runners in the two-hundred-meter race. She and the other nine runners would pass five stakes during the race: one at the start, another at the finish, and three stakes in between. She'd be going too fast to notice them, though. The entire race would take less than half a minute!

Next thing she knew, a trumpet blew. And the girls took off!

Aphrodite's feet practically flew over the track. She

was so caught up in the glorious feeling of her arms and legs pumping together that everything else was a blur. She had no idea where the other runners were—ahead or behind her. How many stakes had she passed? Two? Three? She hadn't a clue. For once, she was completely focused on the race.

Suddenly she saw the row of cute pink flags that was strung across the finish line. It had been her idea to make them pink, of course. With a final burst of speed, she broke through them. Her momentum carried her forward, but eventually her feet slowed.

Then she turned around. Still breathing hard, she watched the other nine girls finish the race. The cheers of the crowd sounded in her ears. Cheers for her! She'd won! She could hardly believe it.

She glanced over at Ares. He was pumping his fist in the air and beaming from ear to ear.

There was a commotion in the stands. Her eyes rose as a row of MOA boys seated up high jumped to their feet. Each was holding a big, blank cardboard sign. At a signal, the boys all turned their signs over. Now each sign had a letter printed on it, and together the letters spelled out: WE LEVO APHRODITE!

Huh? What was that supposed to mean? she wondered. At her confused expression, the boys looked down at their signs. Then two of them quickly switched places. Oh! Now the sign read: WE LOVE APHRODITE! She smiled up at them and wiggled her fingers in a wave.

Seconds later Artemis and Athena ran over to congratulate her. "You ran like the wind today!" Artemis exclaimed.

"You were incredible," added Athena.

"Thanks," said Aphrodite. "I got lucky."

Artemis shook her head. "No way! You won

246

because you ran *faster* than the rest of us!"

Aphrodite smiled. She had, hadn't she? Amazing!

When Hera came forward with an olive wreath, Athena and Artemis went to join Persephone in the stands. As the crown was placed on Aphrodite's head, she burst into tears of joy. Her ponytail had come undone, so her hair was a straggly mess. She was sweating, and she knew her mascara must be running. Yet for once she didn't care how she looked.

Ares was waiting for her in front of the stands. "I knew you could do it!" He gave her a big hug.

"Ye gods!" she exclaimed, pulling away. "I'm all sweaty!"

Ares grinned. "You've never looked more beautiful to me."

"Oh, go on," she said. But she was smiling. Because she could tell he meant every word.

20

Athena

Saturday morning.

I AM A TOTAL LOSER, THOUGHT ATHENA.

Her shoulders slumped as she and Artemis sat in the bleachers next to Persephone. Aphrodite was still talking with Ares near the track below. She didn't begrudge Aphrodite her win. But she was sorely dis-

248

appointed by her own performance. Of the ten girls in the race, she'd come in dead last.

She reminded herself that just making it into the Games counted as a success. No one could be best at everything, and there was still the cheer competition to come. It wasn't an individual event, but she'd still be pleased to win as part of a team.

She scanned the crowd. "I really hoped Heracles would be back by now."

Artemis nodded. "Yeah, too bad he didn't make it in time."

"Maybe he's on his way back now," Persephone said as she snuggled Adonis in her lap. He was lying on his back with all four paws up, fast asleep.

"Maybe," Athena said. On the other hand, at least he'd missed seeing her come in last! As they watched the other footraces, she cheered and clapped along with everyone else, trying to get back into the spirit of the Games. She refused to be a bad sport! Plus, she needed to get her confidence back because the cheer event was coming up fast.

The relay race turned out to be great fun to watch, and she was glad when the Norse team won. They'd done a fabulous job of gripping their stuffed pony's tail as they passed it from runner to runner.

When the races were over, Hera awarded more olive wreaths. The girls who won were jumping up and down with excitement. But even those who hadn't won seemed thrilled about getting to keep one of the stuffed animals. Now no one would have to leave the Games empty-handed, thought Athena. Not even her.

She glanced down at the little brown and gray owl she'd chosen. It was really cute, but a stuffed animal wasn't exactly an olive wreath crown. Not in her scrollbook, anyway!

"Look how wowed all the racers are," Persephone said. "They love getting to keep those stuffed animals."

"Using them instead of batons was an awesome idea," Artemis told Aphrodite, who'd just come to sit with them. "Your ordering mistake turned out to be a stroke of luck."

"Yeah," said Aphrodite, grinning. "Who knew that my screw-up would work out so well!"

The goddessgirls all laughed. Then the salpinxes sounded again as the heralds announced that the archery competition would take place at the range behind the gymnasium in a few minutes. Artemis jumped up and left before the other girls to go get ready.

"That kitten is amazingly calm," Athena said to Persephone after they'd climbed down from the bleachers. "Most cats would be freaking out in the middle of all this action and noise."

Persephone grinned. "I know. Isn't he great?" Ducking her face into Adonis's fur for a second, she murmured, "Did you get used to lots of hustle and bustle while you were lost in the Immortal Marketplace, my little kitty-witty?"

Athena couldn't help smiling. But why was Persephone calling the kitten hers? It was a good thing Aphrodite hadn't heard. She'd run ahead to catch up with Ares. But as Athena and Persephone began walking toward the range, Hades, Ares, and Aphrodite paused to wait for them.

As soon as they caught up to the others, Aphrodite reached for Adonis. "Thanks for kitten-sitting," she told Persephone. "I'll take him now."

"Okay," said Persephone. But she seemed reluctant

to let him go, cuddling him for a few more seconds before finally giving him up. Luckily, Aphrodite didn't seem to notice. She was too excited about showing the kitten to Ares.

"So this is my competition for your time lately," he said, laughing. "I wondered why you were so preoccupied. For a while there I thought—well, never mind what I thought." He stroked the fur under the kitten's neck and Adonis purred up at him.

"Ha! Were you jealous?" Aphrodite guessed. "I wondered what was up with those weird looks you gave me yesterday."

Athena noticed that Persephone had dropped back from the group, a gloomy expression on her face. Hades sent her a concerned glance. He probably knew by now how much Persephone doted on that kitten. It was pretty obvious.

Spotting Pandora as they neared the range, Athena broke away from her friends to chat with her roomie. "How'd the thumb wrestling go?" The competition had been held that morning, at the same time as the footraces.

Pandora blushed. "Not so good? I was dis—dis—" She paused, as if searching for the right word.

"Disappointed?" Athena guessed. That's how she'd felt coming in last in her race.

Pandora shook her head.

"Disconcerted? Discombobulated? Distracted?"

Pandora blinked. "Yeah, that last one! But how did you know the judge in the competition said I was a distraction?"

Of course, that wasn't exactly what Athena had meant. But before she could say so, Pandora went on. "It's like there were just so many things to ask the other thumb wrestlers, you know? But when the contest began, the judge said I had to stop asking everyone questions, only, how could I? And so I got disqualified—can you believe it?"

"Yikes," said Athena. Compared to disqualification, losing her race didn't seem so bad!

After chatting with Pandora a few more minutes, Athena rejoined her friends in the stands at the archery range. The other nineteen archers in the competition were already in place by the time she got there. They'd lined up at a distance of ninety feet from the brand-new targets that she and Persephone had helped Artemis unpack last night. Though each girl would be shooting at her own target, they would all aim and release their arrows at the same time.

When the audience was seated in the stands, the heralds sounded their salpinxes and announced the names of each competitor. The three goddessgirls cheered for all of the contestants, but loudest of all for Artemis, of course.

On a signal from Ms. Nemesis (an MOA teacher who was helping with the competition) the girl archers all pulled arrows from their quivers and nocked them. Athena watched Artemis adjust her stance as she stood sideways to the target.

"Ready . . . aim . . . ," yelled Ms. Nemesis. *"Fire!"*

The girls' arrows shot toward the targets. But before they could hit them, something very strange happened. The targets rose twenty feet into the air! There, like a synchronized swim team, they proceeded to swoop, loop, and pinwheel in formation.

The crowd gasped, and the archers stared in dismay as the arrows they'd fired fell to the ground. They'd completely missed the targets!

Suddenly something clicked in Athena's brain. "Fancy Flyers!" She looked at Persephone, her blue-gray eyes wide. "Remember?"

"Yeah, that's what was written on the boxes the targets came in!" Persephone exclaimed.

"What?" Aphrodite gave them a look of confusion.

"You weren't there when we unpacked them," Athena said. "Artemis thought Fancy Flyers was just the name of the company that made the targets."

"But it looks like the targets really do *fly*!" Persephone finished.

Down on the field there was mass confusion now. The archers were all waving their arms and talking loudly, mostly at Artemis.

"I hope they're not blaming her," Athena said. It's not her fault." Finally, Artemis and several of the other archers put their heads together with Ms. Nemesis and the three judges. At last Ms. Nemesis turned to speak to all the onlookers in the stands. Her large wings fanned out behind her as she announced, "The competition will now continue."

A roar of approval went up from the crowd. "Can't wait to see how they fix this," Athena heard a boy next to her say. "I can't wait, either," she murmured to her friends. They nodded in agreement.

The solution turned out to be surprisingly simple. Now that the archers knew they'd be shooting at *moving* targets, they simply adjusted their strategies. In the next round, they tried to anticipate where the targets would move before releasing their arrows.

"This is so exciting!" Athena heard Aphrodite say. And it was. She'd never seen an archery event like this before! After several elimination rounds, the contest came down to just three archers: Artemis, Penthe, and Skadi.

Athena held her breath and crossed her fingers as the trio nocked their arrows. This was the first of the three final rounds. In each, all three finalists would be shooting at the same target.

As the single target zoomed up in the air and did a cocky whirl, the girls raised and drew their bows. Ms. Nemesis called the signal. All three girls fired at the same time.

The crowd gasped as Penthe's red-feathered arrow struck dead center and Skadi's white-feathered arrow landed right next to it. Artemis's silver arrow, however, hit just outside the bull's-eye.

"Oh, no," Athena groaned. Persephone and Aphrodite groaned too. They knew how important this contest was to Artemis. She'd practiced so hard. It would be a shame if she flubbed up now.

Glancing toward the edge of the field, Athena spotted Actaeon watching the event intently. Was he feeling as anxious for Artemis right now as *she* was? Or was he rooting for Penthe instead?

Her gaze swung back to the competitors. In quick succession, they released their second arrows. *Zzzing. Zzzing. Zzzing!* This time all three hit the bull's-eye in a tight little triangle.

Artemis's last shot would have to be perfect for her to win. The three goddessgirls all held hands and squeezed tight, hoping.

Athena could feel the tension in the stands now. No one said a word or moved a muscle, waiting to see how things would turn out. For a split second she wondered if she should really be rooting for Artemis.

Because if Artemis *did* win, then Athena would be the only one of the four best friends without a wreath. The only one who wouldn't get a statue or a portrait in Hera's temple. She swallowed hard, suddenly feeling left out.

Stop with the pity party! she scolded herself. After all, she had a whole *city* named after her: Athens, down in Greece. Earlier that year the mortals there had honored her for her invention of the olive tree. Of course she wanted Artemis to win!

Leaning forward, she cupped her free hand around her mouth. "Go, Artemis!" she cheered.

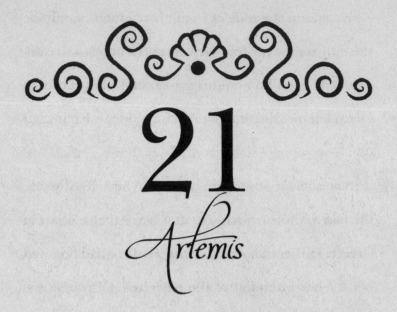

21

Artemis

Saturday morning.

HEARING ATHENA'S SHOUT OF ENCOURAGE-
ment, Artemis glanced up at her friend and smiled.
Then, feeling other eyes on her, she looked over and
found Penthe studying her.

With a crafty grin on her face, Penthe switched her

own gaze to the edge of the field—to Actaeon. Making a dramatic show of it, she blew him a big kiss. Startled, Actaeon gave a little jump, as if the kiss had actually smacked him on the nose.

Grrr, thought Artemis. She could feel her whole body tense as she reached into her quiver and drew out her last arrow. Her hands were shaking so hard, she nearly dropped the arrow before she got it nocked. She was mad! And maybe a little jealous, too, which only made her madder.

Out of the corner of her eye, she saw the smirk on Penthe's face. She looked like she knew exactly how Artemis felt and loved it.

With a jolt, Artemis finally understood what was going on here. Penthe had been flirting with Actaeon on purpose, to try and upset *her.* To throw her off her game!

Well! That plan was *not* going to work. Not anymore. Artemis took a deep breath and exhaled, blowing out the air, and all of her anger, too. With new determination, she calmly focused her eyes on the target. As it zipped into the air in a series of twirls, she, Penthe, and Skadi took aim.

Zzzing. Zzzing. Just as Penthe and Skadi loosed their arrows, the target jerked left to spin a wild figure eight. Spotting the movement, Artemis waited a fraction of a second longer before firing. *Zzzing!*

The other girls' arrows hit in the target's outermost white circle. But Artemis's arrow flew straight and true. *Crack!* It slammed right smack into the heart of the bull's-eye, splitting Penthe's first arrow in half.

A thrill shot through her as excited shouts went up from the crowd. "Bravo! Yay! Epic!" Artemis heard her friends yell. Seconds later, Skadi came over to hug her.

Penthe, however, had disappeared. Probably off pouting.

Hera walked onto the field holding an olive wreath. As she set the wreath atop Artemis's head, all twenty of the fancy flying targets took to the air. They twirled and whirled, their colored rings glowing and blinking. All in celebration of her win. Joy whirled inside of her too. Could this get any better?

As they left the range, Artemis felt over the moon. In spite of all the work and the mistakes along the way, these Games were turning out great. And there was still the cheer event to go!

She and her friends grabbed a quick lunch in the cafeteria. After they ate, they changed into their blue-and-gold GG Squad outfits and headed to the gym to warm up before the cheer competition began. Since all four of them would compete as a team this time, Adonis was left behind in Aphrodite's dorm room. He was so tired from the excitement of the Games, they all figured he'd sleep most of the time anyway.

Before their warm-up, the goddessgirls detoured down a set of limestone stairs to the pool in the basement grotto below the gym. The swimming event was being held here. They arrived just in time to see Medusa ace the race! Though they'd never exactly been friends, Artemis was glad she'd won.

In a swimming contest just before Zeus and Hera's wedding, the snaky-haired girl had given up the lead and sacrificed her chance to become a bridesmaid. All in order to rescue a little kindergartner from being bullied by several sea nymphs. So Medusa definitely deserved this win.

As she cheered with everyone else, Artemis scanned the crowd for Apollo and Actaeon. They weren't in the bleachers, though. In fact, she hadn't seen them since the archery competition.

She would've thought they'd want to congratulate her on her archery win, but they hadn't. Didn't Apollo care? And what was up with Actaeon? Had Penthe gotten him to like *her* now? Artemis's first crush, Orion, had never really liked her the way she liked him. Maybe Actaeon didn't see her as crushworthy, either. Swallowing the lump that crept into her throat, she decided not to think about him.

"I wish we'd had more time to practice our routine," Athena said as the goddessgirls climbed upstairs from the grotto again.

"Relax," said Aphrodite. "We've got it nailed."

Persephone grinned. "We know it so well, we could probably do it backward!"

"Interesting idea," said Athena, "but—" She hesitated, as if unsure whether to say more.

"But what?" Artemis asked.

"Well," Athena began. "Don't freak out—but I'm thinking our new ending might be a little weak."

Surprising even herself, Artemis replied calmly, "Should we tweak it? I think we have time."

The other three girls gave her a shocked look.

"What?" said Artemis. "Why are you looking at me like that?"

Aphrodite cocked her head. "Last-minute changes? From you? After you've been so serious about the Games going off without a hitch?"

"Not that we don't want the Games to go well, too," Persephone added quickly.

"But you practically wore yourself to a frazzle trying to be sure everything went according to plan," Athena said. "So we're kind of amazed you'd be up for making changes this late."

"I know I've been trying to run things and getting all

stressed out lately," said Artemis. "But the mix-up with the Fancy Flyer targets just now made me realize something." She wrinkled her forehead. "Of course, that was just one of the things that didn't go exactly right this week . . ."

"Are you thinking of the zillion stuffed animals I accidentally ordered?" Aphrodite interrupted, grinning.

"And the Pegasus-Chimera incident?" suggested Athena.

"And us letting the cat out of the bag with Zeus?" added Persephone.

They all laughed. Artemis smiled, feeling closer to her friends than she had in days. And that's what these Games were truly about, she decided. Friendships—old and new. She felt the last of her stress melt away.

"So, what I've figured out from all those mix-ups," she went on, "Is that things don't have to go perfectly to work out great in the end."

Persephone grinned. "I agree. Besides, I think those flying targets you ordered added pizzazz to the competition!"

"Pizzazz!" Athena snapped her fingers. "That's exactly what's missing from our cheer ending." She looked at the other three. "If you're really up for changing things a bit, I have an idea. And if it works, I think it could be spectacular."

Aphrodite's eyes sparkled with interest. "I'm up for spectacular."

"Me too," said Persephone.

The three of them looked at Artemis. She smiled at Athena. "Go for it!" she said.

22

Persephone

Saturday afternoon.

THE GYMNASIUM WAS PACKED THAT AFTER-
noon for the last event of the Girl Games—the cheer
competition. When Persephone peeked from behind
the stage curtain, she saw Zeus and Hera sitting front
and center in the audience on blue-and-gold velvet

thrones. The sight of the principal made her extra-glad they'd left Adonis in the dorm.

She looked for Hades in the stands but didn't see him. She didn't see Ares, Actaeon, or Apollo, either. Weren't they coming to watch?

Earlier, with the support of all her best friends, Athena had explained her plan for changing their routine. They'd only had time to go through the changes twice during warm-ups. It wasn't really enough practice, and Persephone was a little nervous. She just hoped they could pull it off.

Hearing the heralds on their salpinxes, she closed the curtains and went to stand by her friends. As each team was announced, its members filed out from behind the curtain to be applauded and then went to sit in reserved seats near the stage.

Only three other teams, each with four members,

would be competing against them. The other teams were from Egypt, India, and China. MOA's team—the GG Squad—would go last.

The Chinese team was first to perform. Wearing sparkly red robes with red-and-gold ribbons that trailed from their sleeves, they flipped through the air like sleek, brilliant flying fish. A few minutes into their routine, they pulled on the ribbons, and out from their sleeves came big red fans. Using them like pom-poms, they threw them into the air, then caught them and twirled them around.

"Wow," Persephone whispered to Artemis. "They're really good."

"No kidding," Artemis whispered back, looking a little worried.

At the end of the routine there was a burst of firecrackers, and the girls disappeared in a cloud of smoke, only to reappear in a dragon costume. A dragon with eight legs. It danced around on the stage and shook its head at the audience, much to their delight. Then it pranced offstage to thunderous applause.

The Indian team wore jeweled headdresses and orange-and-blue saris. Their moves were less acrobatic than the Chinese team, but exceptionally graceful. The complexity of their arm and hand movements, as they wove them together, apart, and together again, left Persephone wondering if each girl might have multiple arms instead of the usual two!

The Egyptian team was every bit as good as the other two teams. At the conclusion of their routine, three of the girls joined hands to form a triangular base while the fourth girl flipped up to stand atop their hands to make—what else?—a *pyramid*!

Finally, it was time for the GG Squad to take the stage.

Before they left their seats, they all leaned their heads together. Usually someone in the group said something encouraging before a performance. But this time no one seemed to know what to say.

Realizing that everyone else was as nervous as she was, Persephone relaxed. A grin spread over her face. "This is gonna be fun," she told the others. "Let's rock it!" It seemed to be the right thing to say because she felt excitement zip between them as the others matched her grin.

The girls jumped up and got into position at the bottom of the stage steps. The first notes of their music sounded—and they were off, cartwheeling up the steps to the stage.

As soon as they were onstage, Aphrodite, Athena, and Artemis faced the audience and went into the splits. With one leg stretched out before her and one stretched out behind her in a side split, Athena was in the middle. Aphrodite and Artemis were on either side of her with their legs stretching side-to-side in center splits.

Together they formed one long line divided in the middle by Athena. With their heads held high and their arms outstretched, the girls waited.

From the side of the stage Persephone eyeballed the long line her friends had made, measuring the distance she'd need to clear them. The first time she'd tried the stunt, she'd run too fast and crashed into Aphrodite before takeoff. The second time she'd barely cleared Artemis's toes on landing.

I can do this, she told herself. *I'm a championship long jumper!*

The crowd held its collective breath as she ran toward the line. Her friends didn't even blink as she pushed off a few inches from Aphrodite's right foot. Persephone soared over all three girls and landed a full foot beyond them. Immediately the other three girls sprang to their feet while magical pink sand swirled high above them to form the words: PRESENTING: THE HERAEAN GAMES.

"Way to go," Aphrodite whispered to Persephone as they passed each other.

"Thanks," she replied as the audience clapped wildly. But this was only the start of their new routine. Athena had rechoreographed the entire thing to mimic all the events of the Games, one after the other!

Next came some comic stunts. First, they pressed the knuckles of their right hands together and pretended to do a funny four-way thumb-wrestling match. Separating, they then began a dance with lots of swimming motions, while bubbles floated upward all around them to *pop* to the beat of the music.

While the whole crowd was still cracking up over

these skits, Athena and Persephone did flips to one end of the stage. Artemis and Aphrodite flipped to the other. Then, while Athena and Persephone held a string of pink flags between them, Artemis and Aphrodite dashed in graceful leaps across the stage in a mock race.

After Aphrodite broke through the flags to "win," they moved smoothly into their next stunt. Athena, Aphrodite, and Persephone stood facing each other to form a triangular base, just like the Egyptian girls had done earlier.

Artemis skillfully flipped upward to balance atop her three spotters. With her friends supporting only her left leg now, she arched slightly sideways and raised her right leg until it was sticking almost straight up on her right side. Then she grabbed her right foot high above her head with both hands so that her body and leg formed a "bow" shape.

There was only one last move to complete this cheer, which was named the "bow and arrow." Quickly shifting to a one-handed hold, she then straightened her left arm parallel to the floor and pretended it was an arrow being shot with the "bow."

Persephone grabbed a round cardboard target that she had clipped to the front of her chiton before the stunt. She tossed it high into the air, and Artemis pretended to aim and shoot at it. Then as her friends let go of her left foot, she fell into the basket of their arms.

Everyone went wild clapping. But there was still their grand finale to go!

Athena looked over, caught Zeus's eye, and nodded. On his signal, Pegasus appeared, gliding down through the circular opening in the ceiling high above the stage. Losing no time, Artemis, Aphrodite, and Persephone grabbed Athena by her arms and legs and, with a mighty thrust, tossed her into the air.

Persephone held her breath as Athena flipped head over heels. What if they hadn't given her enough of a lift? she worried for a second. But they had, and Athena landed just as planned—standing on top of Pegasus's back!

As the crowd roared their approval, a loud whistle sounded from high in the bleachers. Persephone glanced toward the place the sound had come from. It was easy to spot the boy in the lion's-skin cape.

"Heracles!" she heard Athena say. From the delight in her voice, Persephone could tell how happy she was to see him. He was with the missing godboys: Ares, Hades, and Apollo. Actaeon was with them too. How lucky that they'd all arrived just in time to see the GG Squad perform.

But who had won the cheer event? All eyes went to the judges.

23

Aphrodite

Saturday afternoon.

CONGRATULATIONS!" PRINCIPAL ZEUS WAS
beaming as he came up to the four goddessgirls after
the awards ceremony with Pegasus trotting at his side.
Turned out that the MOA cheer squad had tied with the
Chinese team. So all eight girls had received olive wreaths.
Aphrodite was delighted to have two wreaths now!

"I'm so pleased that my idea to have a girls-only Games worked out so well," Zeus said. The girls nodded agreeably. Petting his winged horse's muzzle, he added, "And my fly guy was awesome in your cheer finale. You're a good boy," Zeus told his horse fondly.

"You love animals, don't you, Principal Zeus?" Aphrodite blurted out.

"Of course!" he boomed.

"Me too. In fact, I bet you love Pegasus as much as I do Adonis," Aphrodite went on. "So—"

Zeus's bushy brows furrowed. "Who's Adonis?" he interrupted.

"My kitten," Aphrodite reminded him. She was sorry she'd brought it up if he'd forgotten. But he'd likely have remembered on his own at some point. Like when he started sneezing from cat fur.

Persephone frowned at her. *"Ours,"* she muttered

darkly. Out of the corner of her eye Aphrodite saw Artemis and Athena exchange worried looks. *Just when everyone is in a good mood and getting along well, Persephone has to go and act jealous again,* thought Aphrodite. *How annoying!*

Zeus's piercing blue eyes focused first on Persephone and then on her. "So whose kitten is it?"

"Mine," Aphrodite said with emphasis. Because it was! Persephone glanced at her and then looked away. "Hers," she admitted softly.

You got that right! thought Aphrodite.

"Speak up," Zeus said to Persephone. "I didn't hear you."

"Hers," she said in a louder voice. "But I love him too," she added wistfully.

Aphrodite's heart squeezed a little at the look on her face. She did feel kind of sorry for Persephone. They both loved Adonis. Persephone had proved her affection in the way she'd taken such good care of him. And she'd designed the collar Hephaestus had made for him too.

But the last thing they should be doing was fighting in front of Zeus. What if it made him decide that the kitten had to go? No! She couldn't let that happen. She'd do anything if only she could see Adonis at least sometimes.

All four goddessgirls held their breath as Zeus studied Aphrodite and Persephone. "Doesn't seem fair to give him to one of you when you both care so much," he said after a thoughtful pause. "So I guess—"

"Wait!" Aphrodite and Persephone said at the same time.

"Persephone can have him," Aphrodite added in a rush.

"Aphrodite can have him," Persephone said simultaneously.

They stared at each other in surprise.

"Or maybe we could—" Persephone began again.

"Switch off?" suggested Aphrodite. The corners of her mouth turned up at the same time as a matching smile grew on Persephone's face.

"Exactly what I was about to suggest," Zeus interrupted. "The kitten can stay here at MOA one week, then go to Persephone's home the next week. Back and forth, so you each get him half of every month. An equal share."

"Yes!" Persephone agreed quickly.

Principal Zeus looked at Aphrodite. "What do you think of my idea?" he asked.

Aphrodite reached for Persephone's hand. Squeezing it, she told Zeus, "It's genius. Like all your ideas!"

"Of course it is!" Zeus agreed. The sound of Hera's tinkling laughter suddenly caught his attention. She was chatting with the girls from the Chinese cheer team. Abruptly, he headed off in her direction, but then he turned back. "Just one thing. Keep that cat away from me and my allergies. Or the deal's off, got it?"

"We promise!" Aphrodite and Persephone called back. Then they looked at each other and hugged big time. Friends again. Hurrah!

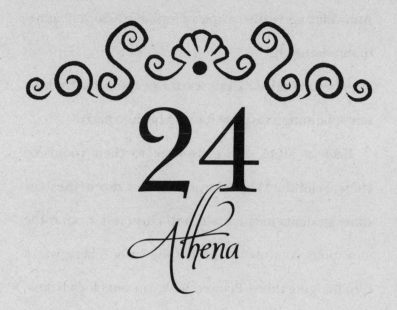

24

Athena

Saturday evening.

DID ANYONE SEE WHERE HERACLES WENT?"
Athena asked as the girls walked back to the Academy. "I was hoping he'd wait for me after the awards
ceremony."

"I saw him, Ares, and a bunch of the guys leave the
gym together while we were talking to Principal Zeus,"

Aphrodite said with a suspicious glint in her eye. "Something's going on."

Athena nodded. "Heracles did write me that the boys were planning a surprise for us. I bet it's a party."

Back at MOA, the girls went to their rooms to change clothes. When they came back down, they saw some students in the main hall clustered around the enormous column by the trophy case. There was a sign hanging there. Printed with uneven block letters, it read:

COME ONE, COME ALL!

TO CELEBRATE THE SUCCESS OF THE FIRST

GIRLS' HERAEAN OLYMPIC GAMES,

YOU'RE INVITED TO A PARTY.

IT STARTS AT SUNDOWN IN THE CUPOLA.

BE THERE OR BE SQUARE.

Poorly drawn sketches of a pair of running feet, a monstrous head with an arrow through it, and a dizzy-looking sea serpent in a swimming race adorned the sign.

"Looks like you were right about the party," Aphrodite said gleefully to Athena.

"Yeah. How sweet of them!" Athena agreed.

"Speaking of sweet, there better be food at this thing," said Artemis. "We haven't had dinner."

"It's almost dark now," said Persephone. "Let's go find out!"

When they reached the open-air domed cupola at the very top of the school, the MOA boys were nowhere to be seen. But someone had decorated the interior for the celebration—using leftover stuff from the Games.

Pink sand had been sprinkled on the floor and a string of pink flags hung from the ceiling. Some of the stuffed animals from the relay races were perched here and there too.

"This is sooo cute!" cooed Aphrodite.

Where was Heracles? Athena's heart sank when she couldn't find him. She'd been hoping so hard that he'd be waiting for her. He wasn't avoiding her—was he?

"Food!" she heard Artemis squeal in delight. Athena had been so busy looking around for her crush that she hadn't noticed the snacks table.

Bowls of chips and ambrosia dip and a big bowl of nectar punch sat on it. There was also a huge, round chocolate-frosted dessert of some kind that was rather sunken in the middle and tilted to one side. Tiny MOA flags attached to toothpicks decorated the outside edge of the dessert.

Athena and her friends gathered around the table along with Medusa and some other girls. "What a lovely . . . um . . . cake," Persephone said tactfully.

"Is that what it's supposed to be?" Medusa asked. "Looks more like a giant deflated doughnut."

"I have a feeling the godboys baked it," said Aphrodite.

"I know! It's a representation of the gym," Athena guessed. She pointed to the sunken middle. "The swimming grotto is down here."

"If you say so," Medusa said dubiously.

"Where are those boys anyway?" Aphrodite asked, fluffing her stylish hairdo with one perfectly manicured hand. "They should be swarming around us by now, showering us with compliments on our fabulous performances today!" She sounded like she was only half-joking.

Only then did Athena notice that *none* of the girls' crushes were at the party. So maybe she was wrong to worry that Heracles was avoiding her. "Well, whatever those boys are up to, they must be in it together," she said.

The girls discussed ideas about what the boys might be plotting as they began busily snacking. A few minutes later all of them jumped at the sudden, sharp sound of the herald's voice as he stepped onto a small makeshift stage at the far side of the room.

Wearing his usual pompous expression, he announced, "Welcome to one and all! Gather around."

After everyone settled in chairs that had been set up around the stage, the herald continued, "The boys of the Academy have invited you all here to honor our MOA girls, who have just finished successfully hosting their very first Games. Let this night be a celebration of them, their hard work this week, and the hands they extended to other cultures in friendship!"

"Yay us and *all* the girls in the Games!" Athena called out. A cheer went up among the girls, filling the room. When it died down, the herald went on. "And now . . . without further ado, may I present to you the phenomenal cheer team—Zapped by Lightning!"

Huh? Athena and the other three goddessgirls exchanged puzzled glances, wondering what was up.

All at once music blared in a dance beat from salpinxes held by two other heralds, one standing on either side of the stage. On cue, a five-girl squad slid onto the stage, their backs to the audience.

The entire team was dressed in black chitons decorated with white lightning bolts. All five had long, wild curly hair. But some of the hairdos were lopsided. And the two girls on either end were incredibly tall and muscular.

"Amazons?" Athena whispered to Artemis.

"Nuh-uh," Artemis whispered back. "All the Amazons are in the audience with us."

"Hit it, girls!" yelled the team leader in an unnaturally high voice. At that, the squad turned to face the audience. There was a moment of stunned silence.

"Ye gods!" the goddessgirls shouted in unison. The squad was all boys!

As Heracles, Hades, Actaeon, Ares, and Apollo began their comic routine, the girls and everyone else in the audience burst out laughing. The routine was full of hilariously clumsy leaps and strikingly awkward poses. But the chant the five boys had made up was actually pretty good:

> *Clap your hands,*
> *Stomp your feet.*

Those MOA girls can't be beat!

Go, blue.

Go, gold.

You're a wonder to behold!"

The boys tripped over one another, lost their wigs, and fell down a lot. At the end of their routine the pyramid they tried to form collapsed as badly as their cake had. They wound up sprawled on the floor. Making the best of it, they came up grinning.

Athena and her friends laughed until their sides ached. After the boys took their bows, they took off their silly wigs and hurled them into the audience. Athena caught the one Heracles threw and set it on her chair. She was going to keep it in her keepsake box to remember this night forever.

The boys were all leaping off the stage now to talk to the girls and congratulate them on their successes. Heracles barreled up to Athena but then stopped short right in front of her.

"Missed you! X-O-X-O!" he told her, grinning broadly.

"Me too," she told him, sending him a deliriously happy smile in return.

He took her hand in his. "Tell me everything that happened while I was gone," he said. And so Athena did.

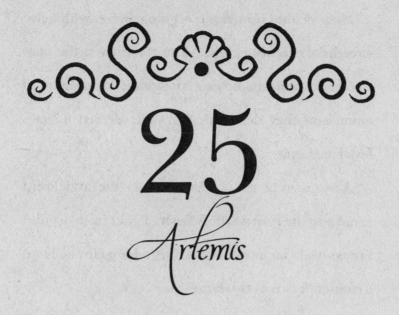

25

Artemis

Saturday night.

AFTER THE BOYS' HILARIOUS CHEER EVENT, it was time to say good-bye to all the guests who were traveling home that night. Artemis joined Athena, Aphrodite, and Persephone out in the courtyard as the MOA girls hugged the many new friends they'd gotten to know during the Games.

Most of the visitors were going home with olive wreaths and other prizes. All of them, even the ones who hadn't won championships, cuddled small stuffed animals as they departed. Everyone seemed to have loved the Games.

Artemis went to hug Skadi when she and Freya came into the courtyard. A flash of gold from around Freya's neck caught her eye as the goddess climbed into a chariot drawn by two large cats.

"You found your necklace!" Artemis exclaimed. "Where was it?"

Freya's eyes twinkled. "Remember Wen Shi?"

Artemis's eyes widened. "The Chinese swimmer with the baby snakes? She didn't take it, did she?" She hated to think that any of the athletes would do such a thing.

"No, *she* didn't," Skadi answered. "But her *snakes*

did. Apparently they love shiny objects. Wen Shi found Freya's necklace in her travel bag just a few minutes ago when she went to pack tonight."

"Since the Chinese girls were rooming across the hall from us, we figure the snakes must've slithered under the door to our room and helped themselves," added Freya. She touched her necklace fondly, obviously glad to have it back.

"Wow," said Artemis. "Her snakes stole it? That's unbelievable!" She heard a weird, strangled cough behind them and turned to see Medusa listening in.

"Have *your* snakes ever stolen anything?" Artemis asked.

"Certainly not," Medusa replied, but she'd hesitated for just a fraction of a second before answering. And her snakes, which had frozen while awaiting her reply, looked a bit sheepish.

Hmm. Artemis suspected there was more to the story than Medusa was letting on, but she let it go. She was just glad the necklace had turned up.

The Amazon girls were some of the last to leave. They were planning to march down to Earth, camping along the way, and then sail home. Artemis was kind of surprised when Penthe sought her out, saying, "It was an honor to compete with you."

Her words softened Artemis's feelings toward her. "Thanks," she said. "You and Skadi were worthy opponents."

"Then you forgive me for hitting on your boyfriend? All's fair in competition, after all."

"Well, I'm not sure about *that*!" Artemis exclaimed. "And Actaeon is *not* my boyfriend," she confided honestly. "We're just—"

"Friends?" Penthe interrupted with a smile. "Naw.

You like him more than that. And I can see why. He's a cutie!" She stuck her nose in the air. "More so than most boys anyway."

At her snooty look, Artemis burst out laughing. "Come back for next year's Games, okay?"

"Are you going to have those Fancy Flying targets again?" Penthe teased.

Artemis cocked her head and looked upward as if considering the idea. Then she said, "No—I'm thinking maybe next year we'll use Excellent Exploding targets instead!"

Penthe hooted with laughter and gave her a high-five. "Sounds awesome!" Then she waved bye and caught up with her departing friends.

"Hey there," said a voice. Artemis turned to see Actaeon standing right beside her. "Good Games, huh?" he said.

"The best," Artemis agreed cautiously.

"Congrats on winning the archery championship," he said. "And your cheer routine was amazing. That bow and arrow thing was classic."

Artemis relaxed, smiling at him. "Your routine in the cupola was pretty *classic*, too."

Actaeon laughed. Then it got quiet between them. His gray eyes searched her midnight blue ones. Was he going to hold her hand (for the fourth time ever)? she wondered hopefully. It was dumb to wait around— maybe she should just reach out and take his hand first. She'd lifted her hand to do just that when he spoke up.

"There's something I've been wanting to say."

He sounded serious. Artemis quickly clasped both of her hands tightly behind her back. Was he going to break up with her? Not that there'd ever been any real understanding between them, of course.

Actaeon rammed his hands in the pockets of his tunic. "I . . ."

"Yes?" she said impatiently. "Go ahead. Just get it over with!"

"Huh?" Actaeon drew back his head as if startled by her grumpy tone.

Suddenly she felt confused and flustered. "I . . . I . . . just *say* whatever it is!" she blurted out. Even if he broke her heart, she'd get over it. Just as she had with that dumb Orion.

"Well, I—" Actaeon leaned closer, studying her face as if to determine her mood.

But before he could finish whatever he'd been going to say, Aphrodite came up to them. She and Persephone had brought Adonis out to say good-bye to everyone, and now she was holding him in one arm.

"Oh, for godness sakes," she *tsk*ed, shaking her head

at Artemis and Actaeon. "You two are pathetic."

Then she reached out and gave Artemis a little shove. It wasn't a hard shove, but it caught her off balance. She stumbled forward—bumping right into Actaeon!

"Sorry!" she told him as his hands flew from his pockets to catch her. "I didn't mean to . . ." But then she stopped talking because Actaeon was bending toward her. His lips brushed her cheek. "What I wanted to say is that I like you."

"Yeah, um, me too," said Artemis.

Actaeon grinned from ear to ear. He straightened again as Heracles called him over. "See you later?" Actaeon asked as he turned to go.

Artemis nodded, feeling like she was in a happy dream. She couldn't believe it. She'd just gotten her very, very, very first kiss. And it was the coolest thing ever, ever, ever! She wasn't going to wash her face for a week!

As she watched Actaeon go, she realized that Aphrodite was still standing there holding Adonis. He was sound asleep, making a gentle purring sound. "Forgive me for the push?" she asked Artemis, her eyes twinkling. "I just thought maybe you both could use a little help from the goddessgirl of love."

Artemis smiled dreamily. "You're forgiven."

Athena joined them, her blue-gray eyes sparkling with happiness. "What a fun day, huh?" she said, a smile in her voice.

Adonis's green eyes blinked open and he yawned. "What did you think of the Games?" Aphrodite asked him.

The kitten stretched out his front paws. "Mew!" he replied.

"I think that means he liked them," said Persephone, who'd come up behind her. She and Aphrodite gazed tenderly at the kitten. Now that they knew Adonis could stay and they'd decided to share him, the tension between them had disappeared.

Principal Zeus's kitten-sharing idea had been a good one, Artemis thought. Just like "his" idea to let the girls hold their Olympics. All in all, things had turned out better than she could've hoped. *Awesomely* better, if she counted the kiss. She could hardly wait till she and her friends began planning next year's Girl Games!

Coming Fall 2012

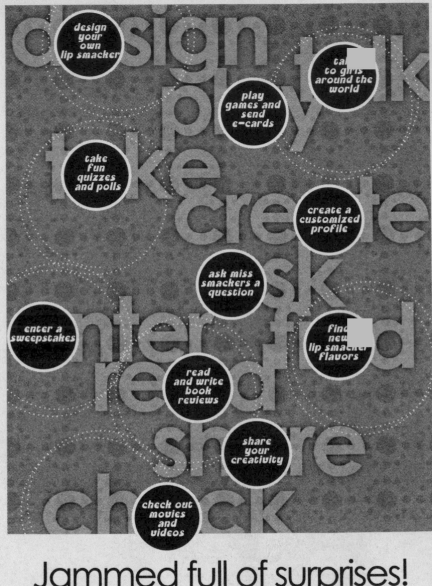

Jammed full of surprises!

LiP SMACKER
L O U N G E

Goddess Girls

READ ABOUT ALL YOUR FAVORITE GODDESSES!

#1 ATHENA THE BRAIN

#2 PERSEPHONE
THE PHONY

#3 APHRODITE
THE BEAUTY

#4 ARTEMIS THE BRAVE

#5 ATHENA THE WISE

#6 APHRODITE
THE DIVA

#7 ARTEMIS THE LOYAL

#8 MEDUSA THE MEAN

SUPER SPECIAL:
THE GIRL GAMES

EBOOK EDITIONS ALSO AVAILABLE

From Aladdin
KIDS.SimonandSchuster.com

Real life. Real you.

Don't miss
any of these
terrific
Aladdin M!X
books.